enamored
CARA WADE

First published May 2020

Copyright © Cara Wade 2020

Published by: Crooked Crown Publishing

Developmental and copy editing provided by Kendra Gaither at Kendra's Editing and Book Services

For anyone who needs a push to follow their dreams, this is for you.

CHAPTER 1

LANA

"*N*o. Absolutely not." I wave my hands in front of my face while shaking my head.

"This is right up your alley, Lana. You've been telling me for months you want to do more domestic projects. A call came in, and I thought of you right away." Eloise Quill, my elderly boss, clacks her manicured pink nails on the keyboard in front of her and gives me a tight smile. I know this smile of hers well. She uses it to seem polite, but it's really her way of letting someone know she's made the final decision.

I shouldn't be fighting her on this project. This is exactly the type of work I've been trying to do since I joined *Quill and Smith Designs* in Boston a year ago. I started here as a lowly paid intern after graduating from Cornell University with a Master's degree in Architecture and a minor in Interior Design and Business. This firm was my first choice for an internship after months of research.

When I got the call that they would take me on, I packed my bags and found an apartment within a week. Dad had a few connections with people who owed him a favor or two, and he managed to get me an awesome apartment in Newton for a steal. It helps that Mom and Dad were willing to help me pay for the place at first because, if not, I never could have afforded it. It's just a few blocks from the office.

I started working with them only two weeks after my last final exam. I must have made an impression with one of the partners because Eloise offered me a full-time position after six months. Now, it doesn't hurt that I was always the first one here in the morning and the last one to leave at night. I've put in my hours, and she knows I work my ass off.

She's become my mentor of sorts, always pushing me into design meetings and urging me to voice my opinions. She truly has helped me get so far in such a short amount of time. This is the first time she's ever recommended me for a solo project, and now I'm turning her down.

"Eloise. Please. I can't take this one. I have... history there."

Why does it have to be that place?

"Lana, I remember seeing designs for cabins in your portfolio when we took you on as an intern, and I've seen how much your designs have evolved in the short time you have been working with us. I know you can do this, and I know the owner will love the designs. Plus, if you already know the place, it's perfect. You won't have to spend as much time out there." She looks back to her computer screen, and I know this conversation is over.

I hang my head in defeat. I slink out of her office, closing the door behind me. My high heels tap on the faux wood tiles beneath my feet as I find my way back to my seat. I'm almost there when Miles Henderson, the office flirt, steps out from his cube, stopping me in my tracks. I really don't have time to deal with him right now.

I give a quiet sigh as my hazel eyes flutter closed for a

moment. "What do you want, Miles? I don't have the time right now."

He rests his outstretched arm on the top of the cubicle, his fingers grazing my bare arm. He's not a bad looking guy. He's about five-eleven, with thick blond hair and blue eyes. He's not the most muscular man I've met, but he's fit and works on keeping in shape. I've got to hand it to him though; the man knows how to dress. He always wears a stylish suit and pulls off the look with ease.

He was here when I first started but was new himself, only starting a month before me. From the moment I saw him, I was floored. He shows up every day in a pair of perfectly fitted slacks and a button-down shirt—no tie. He keeps the top two buttons undone, giving his unsuspecting victim a peek at some chest hair.

I say victim because, as soon as he finds out a girl's checking him out, he's on her like a dog in heat. Always trying to get his rocks off in some pretty thing.

"I wondered if you'd want to get a drink with me later? There's a place I found that has amazing wings—best in Boston." He flashes me a smile, showcasing his perfectly straight and white teeth.

Now, here's the thing. Since I started working here, I have been too busy to date. And I'm not talking about finding a boyfriend. I mean, I've been too busy to even take the time to meet a guy for dinner, or hell—drinks. I put in long hours and crash hard when I get home. I don't even remember what it's like to have any time to myself, much less to have someone between my legs.

It's been almost a year and a half since I last slept with a man. The most recent mistake of my life was Joe DiMatto. Before you say anything, we didn't date in high school. I told him off and spent my senior year back with my old group of friends. Bethany and I still talked, but it was a secret friendship. We're still friends today, and we see each other from time to time. Usually, when I go home to visit Mom and Dad.

Anyway, back to Joe. We met up again during the last year of my graduate program, and it was a drunken, stupid night. I never in a million years expected to see him in Boston, so I was surprised when he sidled up next to me and told me how much he'd missed me. One thing led to another, and I woke up in his bed the next morning.

The walk of shame has never been more embarrassing than through an oversized apartment with his personal chef cooking breakfast. He took one look at me and grinned, knowing exactly what I was doing. Then he handed me a muffin on my way out.

The only positive thing about my walk of shame is that it was the best damn muffin I've ever had.

I turn Miles's request over in my mind. He's not a bad looking guy, and it would be nice to get laid sometime this year. Gotta go out to get laid, after all. It's also the best wings in Boston. Only a fool would turn down good wings. I don't have to sleep with him.

I sigh. "Sure, Miles. I'd like that."

He smiles triumphantly. "I'll come by your cube at five, and we can go. It's not too far." He rakes his eyes over my body and down to my four-inch heels. "You gonna be okay walking in those?"

"I'll be fine." I have the urge to snap my fingers at him like he's a dog. *Bad dog!* You don't need to stare at me like I'm a hunk of meat. Instead, I turn on my heel and scatter as fast as my high heels will take me.

We stumble through Miles's front door, and he drops his keys on a table somewhere, never breaking our kiss. His hands roam freely over my body, and when he stops at my ass, he squeezes and pulls me flush with his erection—which isn't much. I push the disappointment away and focus on his kiss. It's not bad, a little aggressive, and we've clacked teeth a few times, but I've had worse.

He squeezes my ass again, and my fuzzy head begins to clear. I put my hands up and push on his shoulders. "Wait, Miles." He pulls back and looks me dead in the eye. "I can't do this. It's not right."

He huffs. "Just close your eyes. You want this as bad as I do."

Did he really just say that? His words are sobering. I step away from him, my anger rising more by the minute. "Excuse me?"

He huffs again and rolls his eyes. "Just go with it. You clearly need to get laid. You're so uptight at work. This will help loosen you up." He goes back in for a kiss, and I get my hand between us just in time. He squishes his face into my hand, and I push him back, watching as he stumbles a few steps in his buzzed state.

I'm out his front door and down the hall in seconds as he calls for me to come back. Yeah, like that's going to happen. I call for a ride and wait patiently outside for the black sedan to pull up along the curb. My phone rings with a text as I close the door behind me and confirm my address with the driver.

Miles: *Your loss, ice queen.*

I don't even give him the satisfaction of a response. I dial Bethany's number, and after a few rings, it goes to voicemail.

"Hey, Beth. Just checking in with you. Tried to put myself out there tonight, but he turned out to be an asshole with a small dick just like the rest of them. Hope you're having a good night. We'll talk soon."

The driver pulls up to my apartment, and I can't get out of the pot-smelling car fast enough. I look up to my lonely, dark apartment before climbing the stairs to the second floor. I kick my shoes off when I get inside and sigh in relief. My aching toes can finally stretch after being jammed in the heels for so long. I strip out of my dress and pull on my comfortable shorts and a tank top.

I crawl into bed with my laptop and open the web browser, searching for *Black Stallion Ranch*. The pictures showcased on the website bring back a sense of nostalgia. It looks exactly the same as it did ten years ago. Memories flood back to me like a tsunami—the horses, the field, Tristan.

Tristan.

I haven't thought of him in years. When my family arrived back in Connecticut, I locked myself in my room for a week, barely eating. I didn't want to feel, and I didn't want to be bothered. Bethany was the first to get me to come out of my room. She threatened to pick me up and drop me in the pool just to make me do something. It took me months to get over him and the way he abandoned me. No wonder I was valedictorian my senior year. I was so depressed I threw myself into my studies.

I followed his football games through the University of Wyoming's website and tried to stay on top of what he was up to. Every time his team won, I'd internally send him a message of congratulations. And every time they lost, I'd pretend I was there to hug him. It was a silly fantasy, but it helped ease some of the pain I was feeling. I had left my heart in Wyoming.

Shaking my head, I click through the site, gathering as much information as I can. There's no mention of who the owners are, but there is a small blurb under *about us* stating it's being operated under new management. *I might not have to see him at all!* This might not be so bad. Eloise hasn't given me the paperwork yet, so I don't know who she's been speaking with.

Then a thought hits me: Tristan poured his heart and soul into the ranch. It was his dream to run it one day. If it's under new management, he lost the dream. My heart breaks a little at the thought. I pull up Facebook and search for his name under people. You wouldn't believe how many people are named Tristan Ellis. I click on every picture that doesn't show a person in hopes of finding him, but no profile seems to fit.

I lie back and let my mind wander again. It's been so long since I've allowed myself to relive the happy memories and our 'lessons'. Damn, he really was the most amazing lover. I've tried to heed his advice over the years and make sure the guy takes care of me, but most of them don't care. The amount of times I had to get myself off after they fell asleep is almost embarrassing.

Just one time couldn't hurt. I reach my fingers under my shorts and panties, thinking of Tristan.

CHAPTER 2

TRISTAN

*E*loise is going to be here in a few hours. Her plane is supposed to land at ten, so I sent Holden to pick her up with the instructions to be on his best behavior. Holden purchased the ranch with me after my family suffered some financial hardships. He had a trust that was set up in his name, and at the ripe age of twenty-one, he cashed it in.

I, of course, convinced him to buy into the ranch so we wouldn't lose it. This place is his second home, and after a little begging on my part, he spent his money on the ranch. Mom and Dad still live in the house, but with Mom in recovery, she's not able to do as much as she used to. I moved into my own place a few years ago, but I keep stuff here in case. The last few years around here have been really tough, and guests aren't coming as frequently as I'd like to see. Expanding the ranch is going to change that, though.

I'm sitting in my usual spot on the porch, looking over the guest list for this coming week. We have two families with two kids each and a couple on their honeymoon coming. I sigh, taking a sip of my coffee. Ten people total. We used to be full every summer. Now, we're lucky to stay at half-capacity, and don't even get me started on the winter months.

Mom steps outside with her favorite purple floral mug of tea, her frail body falling gently into the seat beside me. She looks like she's aged twenty years in the last five, even though she is only fifty-six. Chemo has taken a lot out of her, but she never complains. Not once. She always has a smile on her face, even on the bad days. She doesn't want me to worry is what she always says.

Too late for that one. I've been worried about her since the doctors first told us her diagnosis. I found a way to be there, alongside her and my dad for every appointment.

"How ya feeling, Mom?"

"Today's a good day. I'd like to sit out in the field and watch the horses graze for a little."

I nod. "I'll drive you out in a little while."

Wild horses have started living on the property again. A herd came in a few years ago when everything was going south and the steady income from guests was receding. Mom says they're a gift from Grandpa to help keep everything going. We opened the field up to the public, so others are able to watch these animals. For a small fee, we will drive a group out to the area to watch and hang out. They can even bring some food for a picnic if they want.

It has been a big hit with tourists who aren't staying on the ranch to watch wild horses. We also opened a small gift shop in one of the unused cabins to sell Black Stallion Ranch branded stuff—t-shirts, mugs, magnets. We've been selling these items for a little over a year now. Kasey got into photography while she was in school in California and has taken pictures of the herd to sell as well. Those sell really well, especially through the website.

Yup, the ranch has come a long way in a few years, and I

hope, by updating the cabins and making them more modern, we can bring more people in. After doing some research, it seems *Quill and Smith Designs* is exactly the type of design firm we need working with us. There were several cheaper places in the running, but I don't want to skimp on this. Sometimes, you have to pay a premium for quality.

I say good morning to a few people carrying bags with merchandise and smile to myself. I finish the paperwork I need to do and help arrange rides for some of the couples staying with us. There's never a dull moment here on the ranch.

Jeff jogs into view. "Hey, Tristan, can you help me saddle some of the horses? The Carringtons want to take a ride, and I said I'd go with them."

The Carringtons.

One and the same, the Carringtons plan a visit with us every few years. Thank God it's not consecutively. The first few years were rough. Russ would brag how he was still in contact with Lana and what she had been up to. It was torture listening to him, but it was like a drug—I couldn't help myself.

It made me feel worse when I couldn't stop myself from asking questions. The smug look on his face was enough to make my stomach churn. I wanted, no, *needed* to know she was happy living her life without me in it. After what I did to her, I don't deserve to know about her life. I know it. But Russ was my glimmer of hope in the storm, and I clung on tight.

The worst was six years ago. That was the last year he came with his family. Lana went on a trip to England to visit his family, and I had to listen to Russ drone on about how wonderful it was to see her and how hot she looked. He got to spend two weeks with her, and according to him, *she's great.* He didn't elaborate on what he meant, and I pray he didn't mean in bed. The thought of that prick's dick close to her made me lose my mind. Holden had to talk me off that ledge.

She was great in bed, though. I made damn sure of that. For the short time we were together, she was everything a man could want and more. I lost track of the number of nights I jerked off to the thought of Lana and the moans of pleasure she used to show me.

Those lonely nights stopped my sophomore year in college when I started dating Savannah. I thought she was going to be the one, but in the end, it didn't feel right. I was with her for three years before I decided to end things. She didn't even see it coming. Not one of my finer speeches, but that's besides the point.

"Yeah, be there in a minute," I say to Jeff. I put my stuff back in the house and kiss Mom on the forehead before walking to the barn. I look at my watch. I have an hour and a half before Eloise gets here. I want to make a good impression, so I help Jeff finish saddling the horses then go in to take a shower.

My phone is buzzing off the hook when I step out of the shower. I rub the dark blue terry cloth over my short brown locks and pick it up.

"What's up, Holden?"

"Tristan, who was I supposed to pick up today?" He sounds anxious.

"Seriously, Holden?" I sigh, drop my head, and close my eyes as I pinch the bridge of my nose. "Eloise Quill, from *Quill and Smith Designs*." I hold the phone to my ear with my shoulder and pull my boxers up.

"Okay." He pushes out a harsh breath. "Well, she's not here. She sent someone in her place."

I roll my eyes. He seriously had to call me for this? "I don't give a shit who she sent. Just make sure he or she gets here in one piece." I decide to throw a small dig at him for good measure. "And if it's a girl, don't hit on her."

I end the call without waiting for his response and tug my jeans over my hips. I decide to keep my attire casual. This isn't exactly a business meeting, but I still want to be presentable. I'm going to be showing this person the ranch and discussing what I'm looking for. I pull on a grey button-down shirt and roll the sleeves up to my elbows. I was going to shave, but helping the new guests arrive took a little more time than I factored in.

This is Wyoming, and I am on a ranch, so I decide the last item I need for this meeting will be my cowboy hat. I place it on top of my head and smile at my reflection. I review my notes and write down a few last-minute ideas I've had for the ranch when I see the truck coming down the driveway. I jog down the stairs and push open the front door as Holden pulls up. I straighten my spine and put on my biggest welcoming smile as I jog over to them.

Holden kills the ignition and steps out, blocking the window so I can't see the person they sent.

"Everything okay?" I whisper to him.

She pushes open the door, and one of her black heel-clad feet hits the ground, followed by the other. She walks around the front of the truck and stops next to Holden, looking up at me. Her face is covered by thick shades, and her long, thick blonde hair is softly curled and has been pushed behind her shoulders.

It can't be.

My knees shake as I stare her down, willing her to take her shades off. I flit my eyes over her body, and damn, she does not disappoint. She's wearing a pair of high black heels, a black fitted pencil skirt that shows off her ample hips, and a blue button-down with a little frill around the neckline, showing a small amount of cleavage.

My body pulls to hers like a magnet. I know this feeling. I have only felt it with one person in my entire life. I take a step closer to her, wanting to pull her into my arms and tell her how sorry I am, but the look of disdain on her face stops me cold in my tracks. She puts her sunglasses on the top of her head and locks her gaze to mine.

"Hello, Mr. Ellis. Eloise Quill sent me to meet with you in regards to redesigning new cabins."

"Lana?" Her name is swept away with a breeze. I swallow and try again. "Lana, what are you doing here?"

She locks her jaw, takes a deep breath, and starts. "I thought I was perfectly clear. I'm here because you hired *Quill and Smith Designs* to redo cabins on your ranch. If you would be so kind as to show me a cabin and the type of design you're looking for, I'd be more than happy to get to work." Her words are terse. I see her swallow hard, and I know she's trying to keep her emotions together.

When I step into her space, her body is so close I can see the small tremble of her chin as she looks up at me.

"Mr. Ellis, the cabins?" she asks again, this time with much less vigor.

I don't give a shit about the fucking cabins. Lana Robinson is back at *Black Stallion Ranch.* This is a dream come true for me. I've imagined this happening so many times, and now it's here, I can't believe it. There hasn't been anyone—not even Savannah—who made me feel the way Lana did. Like everything I want in life is a possibility and not a fantasy.

I reach out and grasp her upper arm, needing to know she's real. Needing to know I didn't conjure her in my mind. Her skin burns under my fingertips, and I want to pull her to my body and crash my lips down over hers. My heart is beating so hard in my chest I can barely contain it. This whole thing feels like a dream.

"Tristan. Let go of me," she whispers.

It comes out as a small plea. Her words might as well have been acid, though. No longer do they hold the love and adoration they once did. Not that I deserve it. I remember what I did, how I ended things between us all those years ago. I release the grip on her arm, pulling my hand back slowly.

"How are you here?"

She smirks. "Your ears must be clogged. Or maybe you took one too many hits in school playing football." Holden laughs behind us, and until then, I forgot he was there.

"I hired Eloise to do the designs based upon pictures on the website and conversations I've had with her. I had no idea you worked there." It's the truth. When I began my search, I never in a million years thought I would find Lana. I wanted a company that would make what I wanted. *Quill and Smith Designs* had designs exactly like what I was looking for.

"The designs on the site are mine. She gave your account to me because she knows how much I want to venture into something like this." She looks down to the ground, and for a second, I see the shy girl who was here ten years ago. "I tried to talk her out of sending me here."

"Why?" I ask, alarmed. Now that she's here, I can't imagine anyone else working on this project. She's like a breath of fresh air I've been waiting for, for so long. I didn't even know I needed her until now.

She clamps her jaw shut and snorts. "Because I have some really shitty memories of this place."

CHAPTER 3

LANA

$\mathcal{H}$e flinches at my words and straightens his spine. They did come out a little harsher than I meant them to, but at least he stopped looking at me like he wants to devour me whole. Not that I would mind—let me be clear about that. It's been way too long since I've had a good dicking. I'm in way over my head here. I should have put my foot down and told Eloise she needed to find someone else for the job.

"You're overdressed for a day on the ranch, don't you think?" he sneers. *Ah, there's the Tristan I know and hate.* I'd rather him be mad at me. It will make it much easier to get this job done and get back home.

"Yes. I was expecting to go to the hotel and unpack, and then change into some jeans and boots or sneakers. I wasn't expecting car service." I turn my attention to Holden. "You said you were taking me to the hotel so I could change."

Holden smirks, and I know I'm not going to like the next words out of his mouth. "You're staying on the ranch while you're here."

"No," Tristan and I yell out at the same time. My heart rate spikes, and my hands are clammy. I can't stay on the ranch. There are too many memories of this place. I need to keep some distance between us if I want to survive this trip.

"Holden, we don't have any available cabins for her to stay in," Tristan says sternly. I watch him narrow his eyes at Holden. A silent conversation happens between them.

As if Holden doesn't care, he says, "Bullshit. You know cabin seven is open."

Cabin seven. Seven has become my least favorite number over the years. It holds too many memories—good and bad. It's the same cabin I lost my virginity in when I was here ten years ago. Seven is the number of boyfriends I've had throughout the years. Seven is the max amount of orgasms in one night.

Well, I guess there are some good ones. I'm still not even sure how that last one happened, but if I remember correctly, it was done with my vibrating friend and my imagination. I'm sure Tristan had something to do with that. Thinking of him is when I come the hardest. I blush as I remember that night.

Fucking Tristan.

I shake my head. "No. I don't want to put you out. I can't expense a stay like this to the company anyway. I'd much rather stay in town. It's a better option for me. I need *reliable* Wi-Fi to get my job done." My head spins as I think about having to stay here longer than necessary. I want to go to my room, change, and pull my big girl panties up to make it through this client meeting.

As it is, looking at Tristan is bringing back all the memories I'd rather forget. My body, on the other hand, has a different idea. The longer I stand here in his presence, the wetter I get. Listening to his deep, sultry voice and seeing the hard planes of his muscles moving under his clothes is almost enough to make me orgasm right here—almost. I shift my weight, trying to discreetly ease some of the pressure forming between my thighs.

Tristan scoffs and nods. "Good. I think it's better for you to stay in town, too. Holden, take her to her hotel. She can change into something where she won't break an ankle and then come back so we can get some real work done."

I start to respond but bite my tongue when the screen door opens. I look over Tristan's shoulder to see his mom walk out. She's hunched forward, and her hair holds more gray than it did last time I was here. She looks so frail, and her clothes seem to swim on her. Even from this far, I can see her bright blue eyes. The same eyes Tristan has. I glance back at him, but his face is unreadable.

What happened? Holden mentioned her being sick, but I didn't think it was that bad. Her face lights up when she sees me.

"Lana Robinson? Is that you?"

I smile and push past Tristan to greet her. "Hi, Mrs. Ellis. It's wonderful to see you." I pull her into a gentle hug, afraid I'll hurt her. We pull back, and I look into her face. She's beaming at me. Her smile is reassuring.

"Oh, honey, what are you doing out here? You look lovely."

"Thank you. I've been hired to redo the cabins."

She looks over my shoulder at Tristan, and I follow her gaze. He's watching us like a hawk would watch its prey. His arms are crossed over his chest defensively, and his eyes bore into the back of my head.

She pulls me in for another hug and whispers, "I'm happy it's you. You'll make the cabins look amazing." I'm happy to have her vote of confidence. She places her arm around my waist and holds me against her side. "Tristan, why don't you let Lana get settled in?"

Holden jogs up the steps and extends his hand for her to

take, leading her to the truck. Then, he pulls my suitcase out of the truck bed and plops it next to me. I try to protest, but Tristan grabs the handle and pulls it behind him.

"Hey, wait!" I call after him, trying to walk on the dirt path.

"Should have worn different shoes, princess," he calls over his shoulder, not slowing down.

I take my shoes off and pull on the folded-up pair of flats in my purse. I jog and catch up to him a few moments later. He glances down at my footwear and shakes his head.

I toss my arms up in annoyance. "What? What could I have *possibly* done to offend you now?"

"Nothing. Come on. Let me show you to your cabin. You can change into something more suited for the ranch, and we can talk about what I want."

What I want is to slap you so hard your head spins. I smirk as I picture myself doing it. Slapping him as hard as I can, putting all my anger and confusion from ten years ago into it. I hope it hurts like a bitch, too.

We walk in silence the rest of the way, and when he pushes open the front door to the cabin, it's like a time warp. I'm an eighteen-year-old girl again. Everything is exactly how I remember it, with the exception of the couch and curtains. Those have been updated.

I suck in a deep breath as I cross the threshold, feeling as if I'm going to faint. The familiar scent of the wood and ranch permeates the air, bringing me back in time. Tears pick my eyes, and I look up at the ceiling, trying to keep my emotions in check. *You're a badass. Badasses don't cry!* I take my suitcase and drag it to the room my parents stayed in. Not a chance in hell I am staying in my old room again.

"I'll meet you at the main house in thirty minutes. Is there Wi-Fi, or will I need my notepad instead?" I start unpacking my stuff, not giving him a second glance. He stands in the doorway, watching me. I can feel his eyes boring into me. I fight the urge to turn and look at him as goosebumps form across my body.

"Wi-Fi works, princess." He leaves without another word. *I hate that fucking nickname all ready.*

I change into jeans and a t-shirt and pull my chucks on. I sling my laptop bag over my arm and head back toward the main house. I replay our initial interlude and bite the inside of my cheek to keep from screaming in frustration. He has *no* right to be mad at me. As I pass the barn, I hear a couple talking over the sound of the horses. I stop dead in my tracks when I recognize the woman's voice. *It can't be!*

I pop my head around the corner and see Mr. and Mrs. Carrington, then hide as quickly as I can. I don't want them to see me. Russ has been trying to get into my pants for the past few years. I went to visit him for a two-week trip, and the entire time he was hitting on me. I may have given him a pity make-out session because I was sick of seeing him try so hard. Really, it was kind of pathetic.

I couldn't wait to go home and get away from him. Our conversations are limited now. I usually tell him I'm busy, and it's a quick hello and goodbye. He doesn't need to know I'm back at the ranch, though, and I'm sure if they see me, they will tell him. I walk faster, taking longer strides to the house when I hear my name.

"Lana? Is that you, darling?" Mr. Carrington asks.

I turn and look back, placing a surprised smile on my face. "Hi, Mr. Carrington. Nice to see you. I didn't know you still come here."

"Simone and I come back every few years. It's great to see you. Are you planning any more trips to England?"

I shake my head. "No, work is keeping me busy for now."

I tell them about my job and how I am here on a work

assignment. Simone and James seem interested in the interior design part of my job, and she even asks if I would be willing to send some designs her way. I dig out a business card and tell her to check out the website. If she's truly interested in services *Quill and Smith Designs* can provide, she can work with them directly.

Tristian is walking toward us but stops in his tracks when she says, "We'll tell Russell we saw you and said hello."

My eyes focus on him. I want to see him in the same pain he left me in ten years ago. Pulling out my best acting card, I respond in the sweetest voice I can muster. "That would be great. I miss having chats with him. It's been too long. I'm sorry to run, but Tristan is waiting for me." I motion to where he's standing, unmoving. I see the tick in his jaw and smile to myself.

I wave as I pass him on my way to the house. He catches up a moment later, and I keep my eyes trained down, watching his lean legs as he stays beside me.

"If I can't expect you to be punctual, I'm not sure this arrangement is going to work," he quips. It's like a jab to the gut, and it's not going to fly.

"I assume you don't want me to be rude to the guests that seem to visit here often. Unless you prefer for me to tell them what an asshole you truly are, and I'd be more than happy to do that." I risk a glance at him. He narrows his eyes at me and looks away.

"The only asshole is their son," he mumbles.

Tristan has never liked Russ. Why would I assume he would like him now, after all this time? Just to dig my claws in a little deeper, I say, "At least he didn't leave me for dead in a field." Anger flashes across his features. I feel it in the air around us; it's suffocating. He opens his mouth to say something, and I hold my palm up, stopping him. "Tristan, you've hired me for a job. Let's keep this professional, and we'll both get through it alive. I don't need to rehash the past. What's done is done."

"You never gave me a chance to explain."

"Your note said enough." I take a seat at the picnic table and open my laptop, ending the conversation. "Tell me what you want."

He tells me all the things he wants done with the cabins— new window treatments, new furniture, wall decorations, et cetera. Then he gets into the fun parts—expansions. He wants to build another set of cabins that can be used as a bed and breakfast sort of experience. The guests that choose to use this option will have use of the land for hiking, swimming, and lodging, but will not have an all-inclusive experience like those staying for a week.

He's animated, and his smile is infectious as he talks about his plans for the future. He reminds me so much of the boy I fell for all those years ago, especially when his chestnut locks fall over his eyes and he pushes it away. I hate to be the one to burst his bubble. "Okay, so I have a question. After you build these cabins, how will you know if the guests are doing the full experience or just a few nights' stay?"

"Each person who is here for the total package needs to give their cabin number. Cabins one through seven are the all-inclusive ones, and the other rooms will be single stays. If they want to experience some of the other activities the ranch has to offer, they can pay extra for it. Hiking, fishing, and swimming are all included. Horseback riding, hiking tours, and boat rentals are extra."

"What about food? You mentioned a bed and breakfast setting. That usually includes breakfast. Are you including the other meals?"

His smile fades. "You think this idea sucks that much, huh?"

Shit. I'm really not trying to make him feel bad; I want to make sure he's thought of every situation. This isn't normal in these types of meetings. Normally, whatever the client says they are doing, we push forward and give them their dream design. I know how much this place means to him and his family, though, and I want to make sure he does what's best for the ranch and the business.

I open my mouth to say something, and he cuts me off, leaning forward so his upper body is stretched across the picnic table. I can smell his intoxicating scent, and I want to fist his shirt and pull him to me for a brutal kiss. I lick my lips. His eyes roam down to the motion, and he stares at me. His eyes darken, and for a moment, I think it might be in lust until he opens his mouth.

"Do me a favor. Don't tell me how to run my ranch." He keeps his voice low and level, but the meaning is clear. *Don't fuck with me.*

I take a deep, shaky breath. "Message received. I have enough to start working on the designs. I'll show you some later, and we can discuss." I close my laptop and pack my items. I need to get away from this man. Just when we start falling into old habits, I'm reminded that he's not the same man I fell in love with.

Walking back to the cabin, I drop my stuff off and look around. It's too nice outside to stay cooped up in this cabin. I grab my sketchpad and decide I need some fresh air to get the creative juices flowing. First stop—the pond.

I meander down the familiar path to the pier that overlooks the water. Off in the distance, I notice a few horses drinking, and I smile as I watch them. There must be some guests out for a ride. I sit cross-legged on the pier and open the pad, placing it in my lap. I drew the basic layout on the plane, so now it's a matter of filling in all the details Tristan said he wants.

I'm hard at work, bent over my project when my phone rings. It's unexpected, and I'm startled by the noise. *Looks like they finally fixed the service problem.* Eloise's name lights up the large touch screen, and I slide the accept button up.

"Hi, Eloise. How are you?"

"Fine. How's the ranch? Have you met with Tristan Ellis yet?"

I sigh. "Yes. He's given me ideas on what he wants, and I am working on a design as we speak. It's pretty straight forward. He wants the expansion to be garden style rooms built into a large cabin. He also wants to redesign the old cabins. New window treatments, layouts, and furniture." I pause, and my chin quivers as I try to get the next words out. "I don't think it's a good idea I'm here. Remember how I said I have history here?"

"Yes, I remember."

"Well, he's still here."

CHAPTER 4

TRISTAN

$\mathcal{T}$he meeting did not go as expected. I run my fingers through my hair, tugging on the ends in frustration. I don't know how I expected it to go. I guess I thought she was going to be excited about my idea. *No, I thought she would act like she did ten years ago when I first told her about owning the ranch.* I wanted her hazel eyes to light up in excitement, and for her to tell me it's the most amazing idea she's heard.

Fuck.

My real problem is I'm so caught off guard with her being here. I expected some uppity Boston woman with a flair for design, not the one girl who can bring me to my knees with a simple look. She can't be here. It's going to ruin everything. She's going to ruin me. I can still smell her sweet scent. It's different than it was last time, her natural scent covered by some perfume. But I can still smell her under it. I remember her essence. It doesn't make any sense.

Holden sits in a chair next to me, waiting for me to say something. I want to wring his neck for asking her to stay, but I also don't want her to stay anywhere else, so I'm grateful he opened his big mouth. When I keep quiet, he dares to speak first. "How'd it go?"

I glance at him, seeing the shit-eating grin plastered on his face. I roll my eyes and shake my head. "I never thought I'd see her again in a million years. I figured she'd be dating some pompous asshole, planning her wedding by now." I look out into the driveway, staring at nothing as I contemplate telling him the next part. "I can't do this, Holden. I can't have her so close to me and not be able to do a damn thing about it. Why did you ask her to stay?"

"Tristan, I saw how much this girl ruined you. I know you were trying to do what's best for her, but it killed you in the process. I hoped that, if she stayed here, the two of you would be able to work things out. It's fucking ironic if you ask me. You hired a company from Boston, and they sent her."

"There's nothing to work out between us. I did what I was told to do. I don't need the distraction right now. Things are tough around here, and I need this project to move forward without any hitches. She's just the designer, nothing more." I sigh and glance up as an SUV comes up the driveway.

I wave as Kasey parks the car. She gets out and waves back at me. "Hey, guys. I wanted to get some new pictures of the horses and the land today. The cloud coverage is neat. I think it will make for some good pictures."

She reaches into the back seat for her camera bag and unstraps the toddler from her carseat. She bounds over to us, her red curly hair bouncing with each step she takes. Her pink tutu sways around her tiny legs. She doesn't stop until she slams into me, and I pick her up, blowing a raspberry on her cheek. Her giggles make me smile as I put her on her feet again.

"Maddie couldn't wait to see Uncle Tristan and Uncle Holden. She wants to see the horses, too," Kasey says, smiling at the two of us. "Right, Maddie?"

The little girl nods her head in excitement. "I wanna ride one, Momma," she says.

"When you're bigger, baby," she says. Maddie reaches for me again, and I pick her up, holding her on my hip.

Lana walks in our direction, holding a notebook to her chest, and she stops mid-step when she spots Kasey and me. Her eyes dart to Kasey and Maddie, then back to me. For a second, I see the pain covering her features. It's like she has it all figured out, but she couldn't be more wrong. She schools her features and continues on her path to me.

"Is that the girl from years ago?" Kasey asks in a hushed tone.

I nod my head, never taking my eyes off Lana.

She stops in front of me and all but ignores Kasey. She takes a deep breath and plasters a fake smile on her face. "Mr. Ellis, I have some designs I thought you might want to take a look at. Let me know if I'm heading in the same direction as your vision."

"I was going to take Kasey and Maddie here into the field to see the horses. Why don't you come, and you can show me out there?" She looks between the three of us and bites her lip. *I forgot how adorable she looks when she does that.* Snap out of it. She's a distraction I can't afford.

"No, you're busy with your family. This can wait a while. Why don't we schedule some time later today or tomorrow morning to review it?"

I don't bother correcting her that Maddie isn't mine or that Kasey and I aren't together. "No, it's fine. Come on. You loved the field when you were here last time, remember?"

She flinches. From the corner of my eye, I see Holden straighten and clench his fist. Yeah, I'm being an asshole. I need to keep away from her. I need both of us to go our separate ways when this is over. She needs to go back to Boston and find someone who won't tie her down—literally. Because if I ever get the chance to be with her again, she's not leaving my side.

"Oh, Lana, are you joining us?" Mom asks as she steps off the porch.

She opens her mouth to say something, and Maddie interrupts, reaching out for Mom. "Grammie," she giggles. Mom scoops her up in her arms and kisses the top of her head.

Lana hardens her stare at me and stands up tall. She's not going to turn down my mom's request. "Sure. I'd like to be able to show Tristan my designs so I can change them if need be and can get out of your hair."

"You're not imposing, dear. We're happy to have you on the ranch. Tristan hasn't stopped talking about the fact that you're here." *Are you kidding me, Mom?* She smiles at me and feigns innocence as I stare at her in shock. Shock morphs to anger as soon as Lana speaks.

"I'm sure he's just excited about the new designs. I have nothing to do with it." She smirks and raises her eyebrow at me.

God, she has no idea how difficult she's making this. She has no fucking clue what her being here is doing to me and how much I want to pull her over my knee for saying something so incredibly stupid. I'm fighting my feelings tooth and nail to do what's best for her, and she has the audacity to think so little of me.

"Get in the truck, Lana." I leave no room for discussion as I open the bed of the truck and place Maddie inside. Kasey climbs in after her, and I hold my hand out for Lana. She looks at Kasey and Maddie, who is settled between her mom's legs. I lean closer, and my lips brush the shell of her ear. My blood pumps fast as I try to contain my excitement from being this close to her. "It will be fun, I promise."

She turns her head and narrows her eyes at me. "Don't make promises you can't keep." She climbs in and sits opposite of Kasey, looking anywhere but at her. Holden jumps in back, and Mom gets into the front with me. I watch Lana in the rearview mirror as she leans into Holden, smiling and laughing with him like they have been friends forever. I'm the outsider, and it fucking sucks.

Mom is resting under a tree, watching the horses along with a few guests from town. Holden takes Maddie into the field, letting her pick some wildflowers as Kasey sets up her camera. She's only in town for another few days before she heads home to California.

Jackson, her husband, will be home from his final tour in the middle east, and they have been talking of moving back home. Kasey wants Maddie to be closer to family, and she wants to be able to help take more pictures to sell at the ranch. I never thought I'd see the day when she wants to give up California.

Kasey has been good to me. When Lana left, I didn't want to do anything or see anyone, but she was there helping to pick up the pieces. When Mom got sick, she came home to help out around the ranch. She met Jackson here of all places. *Black Stallion Ranch* seems to do that for people. Molly even came out to visit Holden once or twice, but Holden sent her on her way, claiming it was best for her. I never thought that one would last anyway.

I sit beside Lana, pointing out to the horses. "What do you think? Pretty cool, huh?" Holden discreetly stands and walks away, leaving the two of us to talk alone.

She smiles and nods. "Yeah, it's cool. How long ago did they come back?"

"Right around the time Mom got sick. She said it's a gift from Grandpa."

She turns to look at me, her lips turned down into a frown. "What happened? She looks so frail. Holden told me she was sick." Her voice is quiet as she speaks. I want to take her hand in mine but pull back at the last second. I focus my gaze on Mom, trying to find the words to tell her.

"Cancer. Took a toll on us and the ranch. She's a survivor, though. Tough as nails. About five years ago, she was diagnosed. Between doctor's appointments and hospital stays, the ranch began to suffer. People weren't coming the way they used to because we had to make cutbacks. I took over, and Holden invested to keep the place running.

"We're trying to find ways to bring more money into the place. That's why we opened the shop, and Kasey takes pictures of the ranch and the horses. I thought more cabins would help so more people could stay for only a night or so. More turnover, but also more revenue."

She places her hand on my knee, her eyes fixed on me. "I'm sorry, Tristan. I had no idea it was that bad." She looks out at Holden and Maddie, then drops her hand from my knee. I miss her soft touch. "Your daughter is cute. She looks like her mom."

I grin and shake my head. "She's not my daughter." Her head whips in my direction, and I see her confusion. Her face is scrunched, and she opens her mouth to speak, but I stop her. "I didn't correct you, but she's not mine. Kasey's married, and when he's away, she comes back and visits."

"But she called your mom Grammy?"

"Our families are close, remember?" She nods slowly. "There's nothing going on with me and Kasey. We're friends, and that's it. She's very happy with her life the way it is."

We sit in silence as she ponders what I said. When she

finally speaks, it's the one question I honestly can't answer. "And are you happy with *your* life?"

I think back to the past few years. I had Savannah, and she made me happy during that part of my life, and lately, there have been women that have warmed my bed, but those have all been random fucks. Nothing meaningful. Relationships are too much work. It was easier to get my dick wet when needed, and then send them on their way.

When Mom got sick, I poured my life into the ranch. Nothing else mattered than making sure Mom was okay and the ranch stayed afloat. When we weren't at doctor's appointments, I was figuring out inventory and staying on top of the daily activities. I'd been doing it for so long, it was already second nature. When my parents decided to hand the ranch to me earlier than expected, I took charge, no questions asked.

"Yeah. I am. I have the ranch and good friends. What else do I need?" I keep my eyes trained on the horizon, watching the horses graze and play in the field.

"Do you have a girlfriend?" She asks the question quietly, seemingly afraid of the answer I might give her.

I glance at her, and she's picking at a blade of grass next to her hip. My eyes travel down the length of her leg, and my dick stirs. I picture her soft curves under me and the pretty moans that used to fall from her lips. I want to reach out and touch her, push her on her back, and press my lips to hers. I want to feel her under me, pressing her hips up to meet mine as I tease her like I used to. It's torture being this close to her and not being able to do a damn thing about it.

"No, I'm not seeing anyone."

She slowly nods her head, keeping her eyes trained on the grass at her feet, and cocks her lips up into a small smile. I start to ask her the same when Mom stands in front of us.

"Tristan, I'm ready to head back to the house to lie down. Can you bring me back?" she asks.

"Sure, Mom. Lana, are you going to stay here? We still need to go over your designs unless you want to review them back at the house."

"You're going to have to come back for everyone else, right?" I nod. "Then, I'll stay. Come back when you're done, and I'll wait for you here."

I smile and jump to my feet, already eager to get back. "I'll be back soon, promise."

Her smile fades. "Hopefully, you plan on keeping this one."

CHAPTER 5

LANA

*T*ristan's smile falters as the words slip past my lips. *I always keep my promises.* Those five words were uttered to me ten years ago, and I believed him. I believed when he said he didn't want to hurt me, and I believed him again when he promised I meant something to him. But back then, I was a silly girl. I know better now.

Okay, I know it was a bitchy thing to say, and seeing the hurt flash across his features makes me feel bad for uttering it, but I could feel myself slipping into the familiarity of him. I wanted to pull his face to mine and kiss his pain away. I wanted to hold him, comfort him when he told me about his mom. Since coming back here, I have felt lighter somehow. It's like there is some invisible connection between Tristan and me. As soon as he's driven away, I feel his loss.

I lean against a tree and watch Maddie run around with Holden. I can't help the smile that settles on my face. Time seems to stand still here. There isn't an urgency to get things done or be on the move. Everything is relaxed. Kasey sits next to me and keeps her eyes on her daughter.

"Lana, right?" she asks.

"Yeah. Nice to see you, Kasey." *No, it's not.* I hoped I would never in my life ever have to see her again. I only met her once, but that was enough for me. But being an adult now means sometimes you have to put feelings aside and be nice.

"Listen, I don't remember everything that happened between us, but I'm sorry. I was extremely immature and jealous over everything back then." She turns her attention to me, and I study her, pulling my brows together. *What's her angle?* "I do remember the day you left, though." That piques my interest. "He was devastated. He became a shell of himself. I've never seen him like that, and I don't want to see it again."

What is she talking about? He's the one who told me he didn't want anything to do with me. He's the one who sent *me* away. I would have fought for him, for us. I clear my suddenly dry throat. "He's the one who chose to end things with me. Not the other way around."

She shrugs. "Yeah, I know, but it's not because he wanted to. He was told to."

My heartbeat picks up, and I hear my blood whooshing between my ears. She's lying. Holden would have said something to me. He wouldn't have listened to me cry all those times and let me suffer like that, would he? "What are you talking about? Who told him not to?" Why am I even listening to her? She made me feel like I was beneath her while I was here, like I was gum on the bottom of her shoe.

"There was some guy that was here the same time you were. He threatened Tristan. Tristan did what he thought was going to be the best for you." She shrugs and raises her arms out in front of her as Maddie tumbles into her lap. She kisses the girl on the top of her head and nuzzles her nose into her.

I get up and walk over to Holden, who's watching me like a hawk.

"Holden, why did Kasey just tell me there was someone who forced Tristan to end things with me?"

I see his jaw tick, but other than that, he keeps his features neutral. "Because she doesn't know how to keep her damn mouth shut," he mumbles.

"Holden, what happened that day you found me? Who threatened Tristan? What is she talking about?" Is it possible he never wanted to end things with me? Was I actually good enough for him? I can't stop the tidal wave of emotions threatening to bring me under. All this time, I thought I was just a fuck for him. Not worth his time.

He shakes his head. "Lana, it's not for me to tell. If he wants you to know, you're going to have to ask him."

"Holden," I reach out and grasp his hand in mine, "we've talked on and off for years. You never told me anything like this. Why wouldn't you? How could you keep this from me?" He pulls his hand out of mine and takes a small step back. I see worry written all over his face. *What is he so afraid of?* The hairs on my arms stand at attention, and I can feel him behind me.

"Because it's not his place to tell. If I wanted you to know it, I would have told you," Tristian says as a shiver runs down my spine. I didn't even hear the truck pull up, but I knew he was there. I always seem to know.

I spin to look at him, hurt displayed across my face. "Why? Why wouldn't you tell me that? Why would you just disappear on me instead?" I swallow past the lump in my throat. My chin quivers, and I lock my jaw to keep it still and wipe away the tears forming. He doesn't get the satisfaction of my tears anymore. I spent too many nights crying over him.

"Because I did what I thought was going to be best for both of us. Because I didn't want you to get hurt or stop your life for me. I saw how much you had fallen for me, and I didn't want to stand in the way of your life and dreams." He takes a step closer, and I take one back.

"No! You don't get to decide that. I tried for *months* to get you to respond to me. I cried for *months* over you," I yell. "Hell, my parents thought someone had died with the way I was letting on. They sent me to a fucking counselor, hoping it would help." I cross my arms defensively over my chest and hug my body. I glance around and see people staring at us. I lower my voice. "Do you have any idea how crazy I felt for pining for you for so long?"

"I know, and it killed me. I know *everything*." His voice is deep and quiet, and it makes me want to punch him and kiss him all at the same time. "I saw every fucking message you ever sent me over the years. I know how much I hurt you, and it killed me."

My face is red, my blood boiling. I'm drowning in the amount of anger I have pent up inside. I can't hold it back anymore and explode on him. "It killed *you?* You took my fucking virginity and tossed me out like old trash. You left me a fucking note. Didn't even have the balls to tell me to fuck off in person," I scream. Now, everyone is really staring at us. Kasey covers Maddie's ears, and a few people walk as far away from us as they can. *Great, now I'm making a scene.* This is the last thing I wanted.

He scoffs and shakes his head and sneers at me. I see a mixture of hurt and anger circling in the blue depths of his eyes. "No. You're not blaming me for that. I tried to talk you out of it, wanted you to save it for someone special."

I toss my hands up and poke the tip of my tongue against my top teeth. I can't believe the nerve of this guy. He has no fucking clue. "You *were* someone special! You're just too thick-headed to realize it. One too many footballs to the head." I knock my index finger against the side of my head, driving home my point. "I did like you, Tristan. You were sweet and caring, and you knew what you wanted." I step into his space, my chest practically touching his as I tilt my face back to stare into his eyes. "I always knew I had to go back home, but I wanted to share a special memory with you. Instead, you made me regret the day I ever laid eyes on you."

His nostrils flare, and his pupils are huge, the blue almost completely covered by black. I've never seen him so angry in my life. He grips my upper arms with such force his fingers bite into my skin. I have enough time to blink once before his lips are pressed hard against mine. *Oh my God. His kisses are even better than I remember.*

I don't want this to end. I grip his shirt in my hand, pulling him closer to me. I feel his hard muscles flex as he wraps his arms around my waist and pulls me closer. Parting my lips, he takes everything I offer. My body is on fire as I wrap my arms around the back of his neck. He's like a cool drink of water, and I'm in the desert.

He pulls back, and I gasp. My eyes widen as I stumble away from him, and my fingers fly up to my kiss-swollen lips. That was *not* supposed to happen. I'm not supposed to let him get close to me. I have a job to do. That's it. Then I can return home and forget this place for good. I shake my head, trying to get my brain to work again, and run in the direction of the woods. I need some distance. I can't think straight when I'm close to him.

"Lana, wait," he calls after me.

I can't. My feet have a mind of their own. I can't get pulled into him again. I won't survive the heartache a second time. I'm only in town for two more days—just enough time to finalize the designs for the cabins. I stop mid-run and hear his footfalls slow behind me. I take a deep breath, trying to slow my heart.

"Who was it?" I whisper. I can't bring myself to turn to face him, but I know he heard me.

He gives a heavy sigh. "Russ."

Now, there's a surprise. I whip around and narrow my eyes at him. "You're lying." I scoff and shake my head. "I know you never liked the guy, but Jesus, using him as a scapegoat? Real mature, Tristan."

He holds his hands out, palms up. "I'm not lying, Lana. I wouldn't do that to you." He closes his eyes and squeezes the bridge of his nose before looking at me again. His blue eyes have softened, and it's hard for me to want to stay mad at him. "I should have told you, but I didn't want you to think exactly what you're thinking now. I knew, if I told you that, you would think I was lying because I don't like the guy. Can we please head back to the ranch, and we can sit and talk about this?"

"You saw every one of my messages to you?" I keep my voice low, trying to keep the tremble out of it. The mention of Russ is momentarily forgotten.

"Yes," he says and nods.

"Yet, you still let me suffer alone." He winces as my words sink it. "You led me to believe I wasn't good enough for you. That I wasn't *pretty* enough." I raise my voice, my anger returning. My body shakes with the adrenaline coursing through my veins. "You could have told me instead of taking the chump's way out."

All the nights I spent crying over him. All the days I spent trying to get him to talk to me. If he had told me this, I would have understood. We could have moved past it. "What threat did he make?"

He steps up to me, and I hold my ground. I will not run from this man again. He's not worth the energy.

"I didn't tell you because I knew you were becoming friends with him. I sat outside your room for most of the night after you ran from me at the dance. He told me to leave you alone, and when I refused, he used the only leverage he had against me—our relationship. I was naive and stupid to think he could do anything with his threats, but I didn't want to risk it.

"I was going to tell you I would wait for you, that we could do the long-distance thing, but he threatened to expose us. I didn't want to put you in that position. Things seemed rocky with you and your dad anyway. I don't know. I was stupid, insecure. I thought it was best to let you go." He reaches for my hands, and I pull them from his grasp. He sighs heavily and nods. "It killed me to let you go, Lana. The way I felt with you is different than I've ever felt with anyone."

"How?" He pulls his eyebrows together at my question. "How was I different?" He's not getting off that easy. I'm not ready to forgive him yet.

"It was like you and I were the only two people in the world. My heart would skip a beat when I saw you. For months after you left, the thought of your lips anywhere close to me was enough to make me hard and need to jack off. Right after you left, I almost bought a flight to Connecticut to find you."

Now, that tidbit has caught my interest. How different would it have been if he'd come to find me? Would we have made up? Would Mom and Dad have let me see him, or would they have sent him away? *Mom would have helped me.* It wouldn't have been hard to find me. Dad would have had to give his address when he booked.

I stare at him, not sure I understand him. I wait patiently for him to continue, and when he doesn't, I say, "So, what happened?"

"Call me chicken shit if you want, but I didn't think you'd want to talk to me after everything that happened."

"How long have you known I've been talking to Holden?"

I'm trying to hold on to the anger I have for him, but it's fading fast.

"I found out today."

"Tell me what Russ said to you."

We walk back to the waiting truck as he recounts the night he left me alone. How Russ threatened to expose him, not only to my parents but to his as well. He told me how he didn't want to risk either of us getting in trouble, and he didn't want to make matters worse. The more he tells me, the more his shoulders hunch. Talking about this is taking a toll on him.

"I knew you were getting close to Russ, and I didn't want you to think I was saying shit just to say shit. I wanted you to make up your own mind about him, and I hoped, one day, we would be able to talk again. When I was ready, you had already blocked me, and I had no way to get in touch with you.

He takes a deep breath and looks at his feet in shame. "I got to see every desperate message you sent to me, begging me to answer you. It broke my heart, knowing I did that to you—caused you pain."

When we get back, Kasey and Maddie have filed into the truck, and I hop in, sitting across from them. I think about everything Tristan just unloaded on me. As the truck jerks forward and I'm jostled in the back, I can't help but think of what could have been if he would have just talked to me.

Would we have crashed and burned? Maybe. But things also could have worked out for us. All I know is there has never been another man who has made me feel anything like what Tristan makes me feel. And that thought scares me.

CHAPTER 6

TRISTAN

I give Kasey a hug and swoop Maddie up into my arms, blowing a raspberry on her cheek. She giggles and wiggles around. "Be good for your mom, peanut." I place her on her feet, and she reaches her tiny fingers up for Kasey's.

"She'll come around. Give her some space and keep trying," Kasey says as she walks back to her car with Maddie in tow.

Lana took off toward her cabin the moment I dropped the hatch and she could scramble out. I know she needs some space right now, and I want to give it to her, but she's also here for a job. I need to see her designs. I'm a selfish asshole and can use that as my excuse to make her talk to me. I push my fingers through my hair and huff out a breath.

I lock eyes with Holden and hold back a snarl. I want to yell at him; he deserves it. I'm still pissed he didn't tell me he's been talking to her all these years. If I had known, I could have found a way back into her life. I could have filled the void long ago, which seems to have dissipated since her return.

I can't leave things like this between Lana and me. I take off in the direction of her cabin and stop just outside her door, catching my breath. I all but ran here. I take a deep breath, steadying my nerves, and raise my hand, knocking hard on the door. In the short time it took me to get here, I figured out everything I want to say to her. I knock again when she doesn't answer, my patience wearing thin.

The wait is killing me, and when she doesn't answer after a third time, I use my key and unlock the door. I hear the shower running from the other room, and I know I should turn around and leave, but I can't bring myself to do it. The thought of her naked, just a few feet away from me, has my dick getting hard. *I'm going to have a serious case of blue balls by the time she leaves.*

I've had dreams on and off for the past ten years about her body. She was hot back then, but I've seen the hug of her jeans on her hips now, and she's a knock-out. Think nineteen-fifties pin-up but with more modern clothes. She's got curves to spare, and I want to run my fingers over every inch of them.

Before I know what I'm doing, I stomp to the back of the cabin and push the bathroom door open. A wall of steam smacks me in the face, and I can see her silhouette behind the curtain. She pops her head around the corner and glares at me.

"Do you make it a habit of breaking into your patrons' rooms while they're showering?" She glances down between my legs and cocks her eyebrow at me.

I feel exposed under her gaze. I glide my hand over my aching cock, covering it from her view, and clear my throat. "I knocked, and you didn't answer."

She turns the water off and pushes open the curtain, her naked form in front of me, standing tall like a Greek goddess. She has no shame, except for the tint of red I see staining her cheeks. I'm not sure if it's from the temperature of the water, or if it's because I'm here. When she licks her lips, I have my answer. She's teasing me, and when I groan and close my eyes, shielding her perfect form from view, a soft groan passes her perfect lips. My cock jumps in my pants and pushes painfully against the zipper, trying to get to her. It remembers what it was like nestled between her legs, how warm and inviting her body was. I open them again to stare at her beauty.

She steps out of the shower and motions to the towel behind me. "Mind if I have my towel?"

I'm too stunned, looking at her naked form, to react. I know she asked me to get the damn towel, but I don't want her to cover up. When I don't move, she reaches around me, the swell of her breast grazing my bicep, and wraps the towel around her generous curves. My mouth finally catches up with my mind.

"Yes, I do mind." I grab the back of her neck, pulling her flush against me. She puts her hands on my chest, and I know she feels my heart beating wildly. How could she not? It feels like it's trying to jump out of my chest. She slides her hands down my body, and when she reaches my clothed cock, she rubs it. I press my needy lips to hers and swallow her moans of delight.

It's like she never left, like we are picking up right where we left off all those years ago. Just a couple of horny teenagers hoping for some fun before we get caught. She opens her mouth, inviting me to delve deeper. I rip the towel from her body and roll her nipple between my thumb and forefinger. I'm rewarded with a gasp of surprise and a thrust of her hips. She gasps and grabs my ass, pulling me flush against hers as she grinds into me.

"That's right, baby. I've got you. I promise."

Her body tenses, and she pushes me back, wiping her mouth of my kisses. *Fuck.* As soon as the words left my lips, I knew they wouldn't go over well. She grabs her towel from the floor and hurriedly wraps it around herself. The spell between us is broken, shattered. If I'd just kept my fucking mouth shut, I'd still be kissing her tender lips.

"Shit, Lana." I try to reach for her, and she turns her body out so I can't.

"Wait for me in the living room. We can go over the design ideas I've come up with. I assume that's why you're here."

With no room for discussion, I drop my head and do as she asks. I close the door quietly behind me and sit on the couch with my head in my hands. I'm fucking this up at every turn. I'm at a loss on how to act around her. One minute, things felt how they should between us. She was letting her guard down. I could sense the shift. The next, I'm back at square one with her. She's put the walls back up, making it hard for me to tear them down. Fuck that. I will fight for as long as I have to, until she lets me back in.

She sits next to me, pulling her feet up under her. She's wearing a loose top that falls off one shoulder and a pair of shorts. I glance at the exposed skin on her shoulder and notice she's not wearing a bra. It would be so easy to push her down onto her back and pick up where we left off. I let my mind wander as she pulls out her sketchbook.

"I have a few ideas for this place, but I need your approval before I can send it to the main office."

She flips the book open to a page showing one of her designs. She starts pointing out her different ideas, including changing the set-up of the current cabins. She suggests taking out the dining table and the small kitchen area and expanding the living room. This includes new furniture and window treatments. One of her ideas includes adding more windows to the current cabins, but that's not going to work, so I nix the idea.

"You want something simple, so guests feel like they are still outside in nature, even when they are under a roof. Guests choose this ranch because they want the cowboy experience.

Give that to them every chance you get. Those pictures you sell in the gift shop of the horses and field? Why not blow some of them up and add them to the walls."

She's so animated, I don't want her to stop, but I also know that revamping all the cabins is too costly. I won't be able to do it right now. "How about we focus on the new cabins for now? I like some of these ideas, and I think they would work well in the new designs."

She sighs and pulls the sketchpad to her chest. "Tristan, I think you would be making a huge mistake to take the all-inclusive part out of staying here for some guests. That's what made it seem so special—at least, I thought so."

I narrow my eyes and purse my lips. "How so?"

She shrugs and shakes her head, taking a minute to figure out what she wants to say. "It felt like one big family. I knew I was just here for two weeks, and then I was going back to my real life, but everyone was so nice and welcoming. Every time your mom or dad saw me, they would call me by my name. There aren't many places where that happens.

"If you have guests here for only a day or two at a time, they won't get the same experience. They're going to be a number. Those people are just as happy to stay in town for less money than they would be to stay here. They don't care. When people choose *Black Stallion Ranch*, they choose it because they want a once in a lifetime experience."

I hear that same sentiment from guests from time to time, but I've also heard from day visitors who have said they would love to stay at a place like this for a few nights as they travel around the state. I figured I could combine the two.

"Have you thought about keeping it all-inclusive, but offering three-night stays and seven-night stays? The new cabins could be used for the three-night stays, and the cabin could still be split into thirds. People that want the three-night experience get smaller sleeping quarters, but they get the benefit of everything the ranch has to offer."

I tilt my head side to side, contemplating her idea. What she says holds some weight. "I suppose something like that could work. I would keep the price point per night a bit higher to make sure we can cover the cost of food and employees."

She smiles and looks down at her sketchbook again. She continues to show me her plans, and I love everything about them. It's like she tapped into my brain and knows exactly what I want. But if I tell her it's perfect, she's going to return to Boston. I'm not ready for that to happen yet, so I pretend to hate specific elements of them—pointing out flaws in the designs or not liking how the rooms are set up.

I stand and stretch my arms above my head in an exaggerated attempt to get her attention. I glance down at her and see her eyes are glued to the small amount of skin exposed where my shirt lifted. I stifle a smile and clear my throat. Her eyes dart to mine. "Work on it some more. We will discuss it tomorrow on our hike."

She sighs and rubs her forehead in frustration. "I don't have anything for a hike, Tristan. I'm not here for a vacation. I'm here to work. Let's meet again at lunchtime tomorrow, and I will have some new sketches ready for you."

I know she's right. My thought was, I could bring her to the same spot we kissed the last time we hiked. Remind her of how well we fit together. Hell, even the two times we've kissed today, it's been insane. The energy and want that surrounds us is unreal. I know she feels it, too. The way she fits into my arms is like she was made for me. I'm not ready to lose her again. Ten years was too long to not have her in my life.

I know now isn't the time to push her. She's trying to sort things out, and I don't want to spook her. I wish her a good night, and I could have sworn I saw her frown when I turned to the door. I stop in the archway and look back at her.

"Dinner is in an hour, and we have s'mores by the fire tonight. It would be a shame if you missed it."

I don't wait for her response as I close the door. I smile to myself and whistle the entire way back to the house. One day back with me, and I'm already starting to wear her down.

She doesn't show for dinner, and I'm tempted to march over to her cabin, toss her over my shoulder, and smack her ass. She has to eat, and I don't want her hiding away because I'm there. *Whoa, calm down, caveman!* She's an adult, and I pushed her buttons enough today. She needs some time to figure out how she feels, and I need to not be a jackass and let her.

I pile some food on a plate and cover it so I can take it to her. I pass by a few of the kids staying with us and smile and wave as they run to the house for s'mores. I reach cabin seven, take a deep breath, and raise my hand to knock. Centimeters before my knuckles rap on the wood, I hear her yelling at someone.

I lower my hand and strain to listen through the thick wood.

"It's over. Don't contact me, don't call me. I can't believe you had the nerve to pull shit like that and not tell me."

Her voice fades out, and I imagine she's walked into the back bedroom to finish yelling at her mystery guy. It sounds like she's breaking up with a boyfriend.

Boyfriend.

Shit. I never even asked if she had one. I was too wrapped up in my own thoughts of having her back and what I want to do to her. I shake the thoughts from my head and raise my hand to knock again. She pulls the door open and gasps in surprise at seeing me.

"What are you doing here?"

I hold the plate out for her, catching her eye. "You missed dinner, and I wanted to make sure you got something to eat."

I pull my brows together and really look at her. She's dressed in a white cowboy hat, a red sequined tank top, a jean skirt, and a pair of fucking cowboy boots. They look like the ones she wore when she was here ten years ago, but that's impossible, right? She's not going out like that. Guys will be on her the second she walks in.

"Oh, thanks. I'm not hungry." She gives me a sad smile and tries to brush past me.

I grab her arm, stopping her. "Wait, where are you going dressed like that?"

She shakes her head, her loose curls swaying around her shoulders "None of your concern. I hope you're not this rigid with your guests normally. Or am I a special case?" she sasses.

I lean closer and keep my voice quiet—calm. "You know damn well you're a special case."

Her breath catches in her throat. "H-have a good night, Tristan."

She pulls her arm from my grasp and sashays down the path to the main house. Not a chance in hell she's going out alone.

CHAPTER 7

LANA

I was not expecting that to come out of his mouth. Actually, I don't know what I expected him to say. I make sure to add a little more sway than normal to my walk as I head to the house to catch my ride. I pull my phone out of my pocket and text Holden.

Me: *I'm going out for a drink. It's been a rough day. Want to come?*

Then I think of it and add:

Me: *Don't you dare tell Tristan where we're going if you come.*

Holden: *Where are we going?*

Me: *The Country Line Bar. Uber will be here in a few minutes.*

Holden: *I'll meet you there in an hour.*

My ride pulls up, and I slide into the seat, closing the door as Tristan calls my name. I pretend I don't hear him. After this day from hell, I just need a drink and to let off some steam. I don't want to think tonight. I confirm the location with the driver, and we're off, leaving Tristan in the dust.

It was two in the morning in England when I called Russ. He was happy to hear my voice, until he wasn't. I ripped him a new asshole so large he's never going to be the same. All these years, I didn't know. All these years, Tristan kept it from me because he didn't want to interfere with my friendship. I don't know if I want to laugh or cry about the whole thing. It's messed up.

There's a chance things with Tristan never would have gone past a few weeks after I left. I would have been okay with that, knowing we'd tried. I would know it was just the timing and our circumstances. Now, I will never know because Russ stripped that chance from me. I hate him for it.

I let him say his side of the story, and when it correlated with what Tristan told me, I couldn't hold back. It's like a dam burst wide open, and I couldn't stop what poured from my lips. He's smart, and he hasn't tried to call or text me back. I know Russ well enough to know he will give me time to cool off and try again, though.

I pull open my contact list and block him just as the driver pulls up to the bar. I thank him as I step out onto the street then I make my way to the entrance. Music blares through the speakers inside as I dig my I.D. out of my small handbag to show the bouncer. He waves me through, and I take a deep breath, willing myself to relax.

Alcohol. That's the first thing on my mind. I want something that will help me get a nice buzz, and fast. I find a seat at the bar and look at the bartender.

"What can I get you?"

"I'd like a Washington Red Apple Martini, please." He narrows his eyes at me and then turns to the bar to start mixing my drink. He puts a cocktail napkin with *The Country Line Bar* logo on it in front of me and plops the drink down, and a few drops of the red liquid slosh over the side and slide down the delicate glass.

"Thanks." I take a large gulp of it and lick my lips. There is a little more whiskey in this drink, like he knows I need it. I hold my glass up to the bartender in a cheers motion as he eyes me, and I swivel in my seat to watch the rows of people on the dance floor. *God, that looks like fun.* There are at least twenty people out there, lined up, all moving in sync to the country music blaring through the speakers.

I remember when Tristan taught me to line dance. It was probably the best time I've ever had. The way his fingers felt on my hips is burned into my memory. The raw need that coursed through us; even after all these years, I can still feel it. *I'm leaving in two days. Don't get attached.* I down the rest of my drink in two large gulps and put the glass on the bar.

I hop off the stool and walk into the middle of the throng of people. It's like they knew I was coming; a few people shuffle over, giving me space to slide in and get my groove on. The whiskey in the drink and lack of food in my belly is kicking in as I stomp my foot and shake my hips. We all turn around and start again. I laugh as I mess up the moves, and the guy next to me watches my footwork.

His fingers brush over my hips, and he pulls his body a little closer to mine but not enough to make me uncomfortable.

"Looks like you need a hand with the moves, darlin'." His lips are close to my ear to allow me to hear him.

I smile and turn to face him so I can get a good look at him, and what I see is not a disappointment—dark hair, expressive honey brown eyes, and a shirt that hugs his muscular form just right. His biceps bulge under the grey V-neck t-shirt he's sporting. I can see a tattoo poking out from under his right sleeve, and I tilt my head to get a better look at it.

"I'm Emmett," he calls over the volume of the music.

Emmett. It's a nice name. I try it on my tongue quietly to see if I like the feel of it. I smile and shake my hips as the song ends. "Lana. Nice to meet you, Emmett." I tip my cowboy hat at him, and he smiles wide. It's a nice smile, warm, and it reaches his eyes that are shining with mystery.

"How about another drink?" He places his hand over his heart. "My treat." He motions out to the bar, and I follow his gesture, looking at the colorful bottles behind the bartender. I lick my lips, thinking of another martini, and nod. He jerks his head, and I follow him past the people sitting at the tables and on the dance floor to a corner of the busy bar. The bartender comes over, and we order. I take another Washington Red Martini, and he has a Jack and Coke, light ice.

"Never seen you here before. Are you here on vacation?" The bartender puts the drinks in front of us, and Emmett hands a twenty-dollar bill to the guy.

"Work, actually. I'm helping redesign some cabins out at *Black Stallion Ranch* for Tristan Ellis." The man's eyes darken a fraction, and I wonder what their story is. I tilt my head to the side, my curls falling over my shoulder. "Are you familiar with it?"

He takes a long sip of his drink and licks some stray liquid from his upper lip with his tongue. My mind wanders to Tristan and the way he used his tongue on me tonight. How he took what he wanted, made me turn to putty in his hands after a simple kiss.

"Yeah. I know the place."

My phone buzzes in my back pocket, and I pull it out, the screen lit up with a new message from Tristan. I swipe out of it, roll my eyes, and put it away, my attention on Emmett once again. He's a construction worker and, according to him, is very good with his hands. I laugh at his innuendo as Holden wraps his arms around my waist and holds me against his chest.

Emmett narrows his eyes in Holden's direction. "Can I help you? We're having a conversation here."

"Not at all. Lana invited me out tonight." He smiles wide and presses a wet kiss to my cheek.

I wipe at the spot and wriggle out of his hold. Both men stare one another down, and I roll my eyes, kicking back the rest of my drink. I don't have time for their shit. "Emmett, want to dance?"

He gives Holden a cocky smirk and takes my hand, pulling me with him. I make it about two steps before Holden takes my other hand, keeping me in place. I glance back at him, and his expression softens. It's a silent plea to not dance with Emmett.

I sigh. "You told him, didn't you?" I pull my hand out of Emmett's grasp, motioning for him to give me a second.

Like a kid who's been caught with his hand in the cookie jar, he lowers his eyes. "Yeah. He knows."

I look to the door right as Tristan walks through, all tough and sexy. He's wearing a cowboy hat with a plaid shirt, the long sleeves rolled up to his elbows, jeans that hug every damn curve, and thick boots. This is not the same boy I met all those years ago. This Tristian is one-hundred percent alpha male, and my mouth waters at the sight of him.

Time stands still. He doesn't even have to scan the crowd. It's like he knows exactly where I'm standing. He smirks when he finds me in the crowd. Me. His intended target. I'm frozen in my place as I watch him easily navigate around chairs and patrons. A woman steps out in front of him and puts her hand on his chest. Her flirty giggle makes me want to gag. He leans his ear close to her lips and smiles when she whispers something to him.

I've seen enough. I extract myself from Holden and take Emmett's hand, leading him out onto the dance floor, just as the song changes to a slow melody. He wraps his arms around my waist, pulling me snug against him as I lock my arms around his neck.

As we turn slowly, I seek Tristan out in the crowd. He's leaning casually against the bar, a beer in his hand. The girl who stopped him is standing in front of him, but his eyes are locked on Emmett and me. A rush of excitement courses through me as his gaze flicks between Emmett and me and a frown tugs at his lips. I want this man jealous. I want him to feel just an ounce of the pain I felt. Emmett lowers his face so his cheek is against mine, and I breathe deep.

"Emmett?" I ask, his stubble scratching my soft skin as I speak.

"Yeah?" His voice is deep and rumbles through my chest. I pull my head back and look back and forth between his brown eyes, searching. I want to do something so bad to set Tristan off, but the longer I stare at this man, the more impossible it is to do. I don't do stuff like this. I don't make someone else miserable or jealous because I want to.

"Thanks for the dance. I appreciate it, but I should get back to Holden." I extract myself from his hold, give him a parting kiss on the cheek, and find Holden still at the bar.

I slide in next to him. "I want to get drunk, and you're buying." My gaze lands on Tristan. His jaw is locked, and his knuckles are white as he holds the beer bottle to his lips. The girl still in front of him is giggling. He hasn't taken his eyes off me, and a chill runs down my spine. "Holden, switch seats with me. I don't want to look at him." Holden glances between the two of us then slides off the stool so I can take over. "Let's do shots."

I wake the next morning, and everything spins. I try to focus on the open door to the bedroom, hoping it will stop moving. *How many shots did I have?* I try to recount them in my mind. I had the two martinis, and I remember knocking back at least three shots of tequila. Holden made me order some food, and I remember taking only a few bites before I was on the dance floor again.

I toss my legs over the side of the bed and look down. I'm in my bra and skirt, but my top is missing. I squint, trying to stop the spinning as I search the floor for it. I stand, holding my arms up for balance, and turn around. Tristan is asleep in the bed, or he was until my high-pitched squeal woke him.

"What the hell are you doing in my bed?" I yell and cross my arms over my chest, trying to cover myself from his steely gaze. I try to swallow, but I'm so parched it feels like I have sand in my mouth. "Did we..." I trail off, not even able to finish the sentence.

Oh God. Think, Lana. Think! What's the last thing I remember about last night? Tristan showed up looking one-hundred perfect sinful. I danced with Emmett. I had Holden order me a ton of shots. My fingers fly to my mouth, and my eyes all but pop out of my head as I remember trying to feel Holden up and kissing him, mumbling something about Tristan getting action.

He raises his eyebrow as he watches the memories of the night play across my features, his cocky grin settling into place. "Your top was scratchy with all the sequins."

He sits up and pushes the covers down his legs. He's in just a pair of snug, fitted boxer briefs, and my dry mouth salivates at the sight. Tristan Ellis has *definitely* filled out in the last ten years. His muscles seem to jump and twitch as I freely eye-fuck his body. My gaze settles between his legs, and I heat up as I remember how he looks and feels, how big he was back then.

"Lana?" His voice is quiet, a softness to it.

I snap my gaze up to his and am met with something that pulls at my heartstrings. *Longing.* It makes me want to run my fingers through his thick locks, pull his mouth to mine, and get lost in him. I kneel on the bed, dragging myself closer to his perfect body. I trail my fingers up the side of his arm to a tattoo over his heart, and he tenses under my touch.

I run my fingers over the black ink, tracing the perfectly formed letters inside the infinity symbol. *Promise.* Memories of words he said to me so long ago come rushing back. *I won't hurt you, I promise. I always keep my promises.*

I look back to him, a silent question shining through my hazel eyes.

"You're the only promise I couldn't keep."

CHAPTER 8

TRISTAN

*T*he pain and rejection splayed across her features make me wish I'd never said the damn words. God, her fingers burned my flesh as she traced my tattoo. It was like she was trying to burn through to my soul, yet the touch was so gentle. She wanted to know about it. It was written all over her face. I couldn't deny her that. I just wish she would say something. Instead, she nods once, stumbles toward the bathroom, and slams the door shut, locking it behind her.

I rub my hands down my face and groan. God, I'm such a dick. I couldn't even leave her alone last night. I shouldn't have coaxed it out of Holden when he said he was going out for drinks with her. I tried not to go. I tried to busy myself with the guests at the ranch, but when Mom saw me pacing and I wouldn't stop, she urged me to leave.

Then, I walked through the damn doors, and it's like there was this magnetic pull. I knew she was there; I could feel her energy. I didn't have to see her to know she was staring at me. I looked right at her, my beautiful angel, and wanted to wrap her in my arms. Tell her over and over again how sorry I was. How much I'd fucked it up all those years ago. Her being sent here has to be fate. What are the chances I'd hire the company she works for, and that they'd send her?

Fucking Emmett Loney had his hands wrapped around her, and it took everything in me not to march over there and punch him in the face. Wouldn't be the first time my fist has found his face. I was relieved when she left him on the dance floor in favor of sitting at the bar with Holden. I know he's not going to try to jam his tongue down her throat.

Every time she took another shot, she'd stare at me as she knocked it back, all the while Clarissa was trying to cop a feel. She was a mistake one lonely night after I had too much to drink. The whole time I was with her, I pictured Lana. I shake my head, trying to rid the memory from my mind. I'm sure Clarissa hanging all over me is what pushed her to feel Holden up and kiss him after one too many shots. The two of us already worked through that issue.

She's going to want me gone by the time she gets out of the shower, and if I'm being honest, I think it would be best if I left her alone for a little. I pull my jeans up my legs and snag my crumpled shirt from the floor at the foot of the bed. With a heavy sigh, I drag my sorry ass out of the cabin to get my head on straight.

I step into the bright sun of the morning and breathe in the fresh air. There's something almost magical about early mornings at the ranch. The hustle and bustle of the day hasn't started yet. The birds chirp in harmony, creating a cacophony of sounds.

I take my walk of shame, if I can even call it that, back to the house and help Mom and Dad with breakfast.

"How'd last night go? Did you work everything out?" Mom asks, fishing for information.

I fight the urge to roll my eyes in her direction. "No." In an attempt to change the subject, I say, "She had a good idea about the new cabins, though. What if we make those smaller cabins for folks who want a shorter experience? They get to enjoy the all-inclusive part of the ranch, but for a shorter stay."

"Did she now?"

Her eyes sparkle. Shit. I drop my chin to my chest and shake my head. That's the same thing she and Dad suggested months ago when I told them I wanted to build some additional cabins that were split. I didn't want to listen to their suggestion at the time because I was too wrapped up in my own thoughts. As soon as Lana said it, though, thoughts and ideas started bouncing around.

"Let's not talk about it. I didn't get much sleep last night, and I have a full day ahead of me."

She smirks but turns around and busies herself with the table. I wave hello to some of the guests that meander over for some food and even convince a young couple to go for a hike to the spot I wanted to take Lana today. Hopefully, someone will get some use out of the beautiful hike.

Just the thought of her makes me harden in my pants. She was so sexy last night. I'm not even sure she remembers what happened. She practically flung herself on me after doing one too many shots with Holden. She told me what an idiot I was for letting her go, and I couldn't argue with her logic because she's right. I'm the biggest idiot known to man.

When I told her I was taking her home, she tried to fight me, saying she wanted Holden to take her home. *Yeah, not a chance in hell.* I'm not letting him protect her when I'm perfectly capable of doing it myself. Then, I got her back to the cabin, and she asked me to stay with her. She said she didn't want to be alone. How can any man be strong enough to refuse a woman in need?

I sure as hell didn't sleep well with her right next to me.

She tossed her hat and kicked off her boots before settling down into the bed. At one point, she complained about her shirt being scratchy, but she didn't want her pajamas. I helped her pull her shirt over her head, my fingers trailing her delicate skin, goosebumps rising in their wake.

It was the hardest damned thing to refuse when she begged me to kiss her—to take her. She was drunk, and I wasn't going to break the small thread of trust I have left with this beautiful woman. She rolled over, giving me her back, and passed out. After her breathing evened out, I placed a gentle kiss on her shoulder and pulled her against me.

I may have done the right thing by not taking things too far, but there was not a chance in hell I'd miss wrapping my arms around her for the night. I've had this fantasy since she first came to the ranch. She enveloped my senses, and all my thoughts ran rampant with memories of her. Touching her, kissing her, making her moan.

Holden tosses a granola bar at me, snapping me out of my stupor. I snatch the bar from the ground and glare at him as I stand to my full height again. He has a shit-eating grin on his face.

"Hey, Romeo. How'd last night go?"

"Fine."

"That's all I get? Fine? Didn't see you come back last night. Those look like the same clothes as last night. Did the walk of shame this morning?" he eggs me on.

"That's because I didn't. She was drunk, Holden. Nothing happened between us. We slept." Even though I would have given my left nut to get any sort of action from Lana.

I walk into the house so I can shower and get some new clothes on. Holden calls after me, but I ignore him. I lock my bedroom door behind me and strip out of last night's clothes as I let the water heat up. The water droplets trickle down my body, splashing on the bottom of the tub as I think about Lana again. The thought of her has my cock growing to attention.

She felt so perfect with her ass pressed against me last night. That, coupled with the memory of seeing her naked and kissing her tender lips, has me reaching my hand down for a quick tug. It doesn't take me long to work out the pent-up frustration, and I moan as I coat the tiles with my cum. I drop my head and catch my breath.

What the hell am I going to do? She leaves tomorrow morning, and I'm not prepared to let her walk away. I'm not ready to say goodbye. I haven't gotten to say any of the things I promised I would say the next time I saw her. I haven't gotten to apologize properly. I tried when she first arrived, but she wasn't having any of it.

I dress quickly, hoping to meet her outside. I spot her with Holden, holding a steaming cup against her lips, blowing on it to cool it down. I grab a bowl of oatmeal, a banana, and a bottle of water to intercept their conversation. As I get closer, I can hear her talking quietly, so I slow my pace, hoping to hear something juicy.

"I can't believe he would do that to me." She sighs and rubs her forehead. "I need to start over, forget about the past."

My heart sinks. Too much time has passed between us. I really thought she was warming up to me, that today we could sit down and have a real heart to heart talk, and I could finally apologize for being the asshole I was to her. Make her see I'm not like that. Let her see me as she saw me when we were naive kids.

Fuck.

"Hey, Tristan," Holden says.

Lana whips her head around to look at me and winces in pain. She must have a massive hangover today. I hold the water out for her, and she takes it. A quiet thank you passes between us before the awkwardness sets in.

Holden starts to slowly back away, and the sheer look of panic on her face makes me stop him.

"No. Stay, Holden. I'm going to go check things at the barn. Wanted to make sure Lana was feeling okay." I look at her. "Make sure you drink lots of water and eat a banana. It should help with the hangover. Let's meet after lunch, and you can show me the new designs."

She nods. "Okay."

I leave the two of them alone, put my full plate in with the dirty dishes since I've lost my appetite, and sulk all the way to the barn. God, I really am such an idiot! There's nothing I need to do here. Billy has everything under control, and no one needs a guide today. I think it would be best if I head home for a bit. Mom and Dad have things taken care of here. They would be fine for a few hours.

What am I going to do at home? Nothing. I'm going to sulk there, too. I scrub my hands down my face and sigh. I decide to saddle up Gage and go for a ride. Riding has always calmed me and centered me. There is a quiet knock on the barn wall, and I spin to find Lana standing there.

"Hey." She wiggles her fingers at me.

"Hey." I turn back around and finish securing the saddle to his back. I'm not sure I can handle looking at her right now. Not after I know she wants to forget me.

"I, um," she pushes out a harsh breath, "I wanted to say thank you for last night. For making sure I was safe."

"Yeah, no problem." I grab Gage's reins and lead him past Lana and out of the barn before hopping on his back and riding away like a coward.

Her designs are perfect. She's factored in everything I wanted for the new cabins, just like I knew she would. Lana definitely has a knack for design, and I couldn't be prouder of her. I made myself scarce for the rest of the afternoon. I told her I would be in touch with the office about getting copies of the finished blueprints for the builders.

"You know, our company also does interior designing. When the cabins are built, if you need someone, I'm just a phone call away," she says, her voice sweet.

"Yeah. Great. Thanks. I'll call the office if I'm in need of your company's services." I poke at one of the logs in the fire, keeping my eyes glued to the embers that crackle free from the burning wood and float into the sky.

She sighs and stands in defeat. "Goodnight, Tristan. It was great to see you again. I hope everything works out for you."

I watch her retreating form and lean back in my chair. How did I fuck this up again? I try to think about what I did that could have been so bad. Okay, so barging into her bathroom while she was showering wasn't my finest moment, nor was staying with her after the bar. Each time, though, she was willing. She wanted me just as much as I wanted her.

Maybe Holden has some insight for me. The two of them have been very close since she arrived. He's gone home for the night, and I figure it's best to wait until morning to talk to him. Dad is sitting by the fire, and I stand and stretch.

"I'm going to head home for the night. See ya in the morning, Dad." He waves to me, and I head home.

Someone pounding on my front door pulls me from my restless sleep. I need to start taking something for this shit. I pad down the hall in nothing but my boxers and pull the door wide open.

"You're a fucking idiot; you know that?" Holden asks as he shoulders past me into my living room.

"Please, do come in," I mumble, closing the door behind him. "Why am I a fucking idiot?"

"You brushed Lana off all day yesterday, and then, you didn't even get your happy ass to the ranch to say goodbye to her this morning. She was devastated when I dropped her off at the airport. I tried calling and texting you, but you didn't answer," he seethes. "You bitched and moaned about fixing things since she arrived, and then pull this shit."

"Not like she wanted to see me anyway. She couldn't believe how I acted and couldn't wait to put her past behind her. Sound familiar?" I cross my arms over my chest, facing him straight on.

He snorts and sneers at me again. "Yeah, sounds like she was talking about that prick, Russ."

My stomach flips, and my eyes widen to the size of saucers. "W-what?"

"Yeah, asshole. She was going to forgive you, and you fucked it all up. Again."

I sit on the couch and drop my head in my shaking hands. I can't believe I did it to us again. "I need a flight to Boston."

He smiles. "Thought you'd never ask."

CHAPTER 9

LANA

*H*olden pulls his truck up and loads my suitcase into the back of it. I look out past him, expecting to see Tristan, but he isn't there.

"He's not coming, is he?" I ask, deflated.

He shakes his head sadly. "I don't think so."

"I don't know what happened. He brushed me off when I tried to talk to him yesterday morning, and last night the same thing. Did I say something?" *Am I still not enough for him?* I thought we were moving past that. The kiss, the desire pooling in his eyes each time we touched...

My insecurities come back full force, and I do the one thing I've gotten good at—tamp them down. I am a successful woman, and I won't fawn over a man who doesn't want me in return. I'm better than that. This whole trip was a mistake. I should have insisted Eloise send someone else or come herself.

I won't make that mistake again. If Tristan does call back for additional work, someone else is taking the account. I really thought we were going to be able to mend things between us, especially when he clearly still wanted me—at some point anyway.

I give Holden a huge hug and promise to let him know when I arrive home safe. I manage to choke back tears until I make it to my gate, then I can't stop them from pouring out. I've had a couple of people move to other seats, but I did have one nice woman hand me a wad of tissues. I thanked her and gave her the best sad smile I could muster.

I just want to go home and sleep, but my flight arrives around one in the afternoon, and I know Eloise is going to want the designs so we can begin working on them. It will only be a four-hour shift, so it won't be that bad. Then, I can go home and curl up with a good book. I've tried reading a few times sitting on this plane already, but every time I start, I cry again.

Gah! Get a hold of yourself, Lana! He's not worth it. No man is worth this many tears. I pull my laptop out and write down all the things I wanted to say to Tristan but didn't get the chance to. I thought he'd still be in the bedroom when I got back from the bathroom, but he was gone. Then, I hoped we could talk at breakfast, but he ran away—again. It's like getting whiplash. One minute, he's all over me, and the next, it's like I have the plague.

I glance at my phone for the time and decide to try to sleep a little. Maybe if I can sleep, I can forget about him. As much as I would like to, I won't be able to. My dreams have been of Tristan for the past two nights, and I'm sure I won't be able to get his wide chest, strong arms, or piercing blue eyes out of my mind anytime soon.

"Hey, welcome back. How was Montana?" Dustin, my best friend in the office, sits at the edge of my desk and cocks a boyish grin in my direction. He has the potential to be a looker with his sandy blond hair and hazel eyes, but nothing compares to Tristan.

I sigh. "You know damn well it was Wyoming, Dustin." I roll my eyes but laugh anyway.

"Oh, that's right. Another state no one ever visits. Did you get the plans approved?"

"Would you expect anything less of me?" I feign shock and place my hand on my chest.

We talk for the next few minutes about my trip and having to stay on the ranch. I try to skirt the subject of Tristan because Dustin can be a bit of a gossip, and I don't need that getting around. Eloise knows about him. That's enough for me.

My phone rings, and Hillary, the front receptionist's name, flashes on the screen. I put the phone to my ear, expecting to hear that Eloise wants to see me, but she requests I meet her at the front desk. *Okay, that's weird.* Dustin smirks when I shrug and hang up the phone.

When I get to Hillary's desk, the biggest bouquet of flowers I have ever seen is sitting in front of her. This thing must have cost a fortune.

"Trying to rub in the fact that your husband loves you?" I tease.

"Oh, God. I wish. They're for you." She smiles and raises her eyebrow, waiting for me to respond.

I put my hand over my chest in disbelief. "Me? Now, you're pulling my leg. There's no one who wants to send me flowers." I dig through the multiple colored orchids and roses until I find the small card. My cheeks light up in embarrassment as I pull the card out from the envelope and read it.

Lana,
I never meant to cause so much drama. I was stupid back

then. I don't want to lose our friendship over something that's in the past. Please accept this as the start of an apology. I'm sorry.

XX

Russ

My heart sinks, and my good mood sours. I thought for sure they would be from Tristan. The moment I saw them sitting on Hillary's desk, my heart almost beat out of my chest at the thought. I put the small card in my back pocket.

"Keep 'em. They really brighten up the front."

"You can't be serious," she scoffs. "Lana, what's wrong?" Hillary comes around the desk and tilts her head, watching me.

My chin quivers, and I clamp my jaw shut, stopping the trembling. I shake my head and smile through my obvious pain. "Nothing. They're too big for my cubicle, and I think they would look great here."

She narrows her eyes but smiles. "Okay, if you're sure."

I nod and hurry back to my desk. I open my laptop and email the designs to Eloise with a note letting her know I'm not feeling well and will finish out the day at home. I all but run past Hillary and Dustin as the two of them talk, most likely about me.

I take the elevator down to the parking garage, and when I get into my car, I sit there for a few minutes, trying to regain my composure. My phone lights up with a new message from Holden.

Holden: *Wanted to make sure you made it back safe. It was good seeing you. Hopefully, we will see each other again soon. What's your home address? I want to send you something.*

Me: *Sorry, yes, I made it safe. You don't have to send me anything.*

Holden: *Please?*

I roll my eyes and type my address to him. What is it that he could possibly want to send me? I just want to go home. I'm exhausted and ready to crash, even though it's only three in the afternoon. *Must be the mountain air.* I put my car in drive and decide to stop at the store for some groceries before I head home.

You know what stinks about living in a second-floor apartment in the city? Trying to lug grocery bags up them. I bought a little more than I intended to, and now, the stupid plastic bags are cutting off circulation to my fingers, making them turn an ugly shade of blue. I step onto the landing and take a deep breath. *I really need to get back into the gym.*

I push open the hallway door and freeze in place, my mouth hanging open, the bags slipping from my grasp. I hear the glass clink on the hard floor and wince, hoping I didn't break the bottles of wine. He smirks at me and stands to his full height, a bouquet of flowers held securely in his grasp. He looks tired. His hair is disheveled, and he runs his fingers through the chestnut locks, messing them up even more.

"W-what are you doing here?" My eyes must be messing with me. I'm dreaming or something. He takes a step closer and extends the flowers in front of him. They're beautiful, and my favorite—lilies. The flowers are in various shades of pink and white, and my heart melts.

"I'm so sorry, Lana. I fucked it all up, and I'm so damn sorry." He stops in front of me, hands me the flowers, and bends to pick up all the bags. "Can we talk? Let me say what I have to, and then, if you don't want me, I'll leave you alone."

How can I say no to that? He flew across the country to talk to me—to apologize. That takes some guts. I nod and fish the keys out of my bag to unlock the door. My hands shake, and it takes me two tries before I get the key in the lock. We walk through, and he drops the bags off in the kitchen as I find a vase to put the flowers in.

"Can I get you something to drink?" I call over my shoulder.

"No, I'm good."

"Wait for me in the living room. I need to get these groceries put away."

He doesn't argue, and after a few minutes, I join him. I sit in the chair next to him, not trusting myself to sit on the loveseat with him.

"Thank you for the flowers. They're beautiful."

"You're welcome." He leans forward, places his forearms on his knees, and pushes out a deep breath, his eyes focused on the ground between his feet. He looks up at me, and I can see how he feels deep within his eyes. I see the sadness, the hurt, the fear all swirling around like a brewing storm.

"I was a fucking idiot." *Well, I'm not going to deny that fact.* "I didn't know you were going to be the one who showed up, and I sure as hell didn't handle it well. Then, I heard talking to Holden yesterday morning, talking about how you needed to forget the past and start over." I open my mouth to speak, and he holds his hand up. "I know, you were referring to Russ. Holden told me when he ripped me a new asshole this morning for not being there to say goodbye."

He reaches out, stroking the side of my jean-clad leg gently. "I thought you were talking about me and having to forget about me. I didn't get the chance to tell you how sorry I am for everything. For all those years ago, for everything that happened at the ranch, and for breaking my promises. I never meant to hurt you."

I stand, moving out of his reach. My mind is swimming with questions I don't even know how to begin to ask.

"I need a glass of wine." I walk into the kitchen, leaving him alone again, and take my phone with me. I pour a healthy glass of my new red wine and gulp half of it down before refilling the glass.

Me: *Is my present tall, dark, and handsome?*

My phone buzzes moments later with a reply.

Holden: *No, I'm not there. LOL! Kidding. Listen to what he has to say and keep an open mind.*

I take my glass of wine back into the living room. He's sitting there, so deflated. He scrubs his hands down his face and slumps over, his elbows resting on his knees. I don't want to be mad at him. I've spent too many years mad at him. Hell, if I'm being honest, I want to sit in his lap and smother him in kisses, demand he make up for lost time.

"Hi, I'm Lana Robinson. I'm twenty-eight years old, and I'm an architect. I've been at my current job for about a year now, and I love what I do. I also love to read, and my ideal night would be a good book and a glass of wine." I extend my hand out to him and wait. He smirks and stands, taking my hand in his for a firm handshake.

"It's nice to meet you, Lana. I'm Tristan Ellis, and I tend to put my foot in my mouth. I'm also twenty-eight, and I own a ranch in Wyoming. I lost the perfect girl ten years ago, and I've been lost ever since." He reaches out for me, his strong arm wrapping around my waist, pulling me closer. His other hand tucks a stray piece of hair behind my ear. "Will you forgive me for being such an asshole to you?"

The air around us changes; it's electric, full of energy. I can almost hear the crackling as he waits patiently for me to respond.

"I didn't think I'd ever see you again," I whisper, running my finger along his strong jawline.

"I couldn't lose you again. Not like this. Not when I can fight for you."

"If I give you my heart, will you promise not to break it this time?"

He drops his forehead down on mine. "I promise."

CHAPTER 10

TRISTAN

*T*his evening has gone better than I expected it would. I honestly had no idea what would happen or how she would react. Her look of utter shock when she saw me sitting outside was to be expected, but I didn't know if she would invite me in or not. *Oh, who am I kidding? I knew she would.* She might have been mad at me, but I knew she would give me a chance.

I want to kiss her. I want to push her against the damn wall and make her scream my name. I also don't want to scare her, so I pull back to look in her eyes. They sparkle, but there's also a haze of lust swimming around. I take a chance and lean forward, my lips hovering over hers. I feel her breath on me, soft pants as I wait for her to close the gap.

When she does, blood rushes through my body to all the spots I want her to touch. I control the kiss—the speed, the depth, the heat. I don't want to rush into this. We need to take it slow, get to know one another again. I need her to trust me. I pull back, even though I don't want to, leaving her panting, wanting more. She blinks her eyes open to look at me, and I see the raw need there. She licks her lips, her chest heaving.

"How about we get something to eat and we can talk?"

She sobers up, straightening her spine, and nods. "Let me get my purse, and we can go. By the way, where are you staying tonight?"

I was hoping with you. I scratch the back of my neck and wince. "Nowhere yet. I figured I'd find something depending on how things went today." She smirks and nods, forming an O shape with her mouth. "Not that I expect you to offer your house to me. I'll figure it out." I shrug and smile at her.

"You could stay here if you want. It would save you some money. I can't imagine that flight was cheap." She narrows her eyes at me. "How did you manage to get a flight at the last minute?"

"A bit of luck and a lot of money. I've never flown first-class before. The free booze was a nice touch." I chuckle. "I don't want to impose unless you're really sure."

She smiles, and my whole world lights up. "I am."

At dinner, I pretend this is a first date and wine and dine her. I spend the time getting to know her, finding out all the things that have happened for her in the past ten years. She's amazing. There are no other words to describe the beautiful woman sitting in front of me. She's worked her ass off to get to where she is, and I couldn't be prouder of her.

"I know you've been talking to Holden on and off for the past ten years. Did you ever ask about me?"

She offers a shy smile. "Every time." She looks down at her margarita, playing with the straw, swirling the pink liquid around. "When he wouldn't tell me anything, I started following your football career through the school's website. I was desperate for any information I could find on you. I didn't want to believe I meant so little to you."

I place my hand over hers, stopping her fidgeting. "You meant a lot to me. Still do. It took me two years to finally open my heart again and start dating. You consumed my dreams for years." I feel my ears heat up as I think about the next thing to come out of my mouth. "You were my spank bank material."

"Were?" she asks, raising her eyebrow and smirking.

"Don't want to scare you off," I tease. My smile fades. "Anyway, I got updates from Russ about you, and I *hated* the fact you two still talked. It was torture, hearing how happy you were from him. I even found out about your trip to England to visit him. Definitely not what I wanted to hear." I still want to punch him, just thinking about it.

She groans and drops her head to her hand. "He told you about that?"

"Yup." I take a deep breath and wait until she looks at me again. "Did he fabricate it? Did you sleep with him?"

She chokes on her drink and falls into a small coughing fit. She holds her hands in front of her, keeping me planted in my seat until she can breathe normally again.

"That's what he told you?" Her voice is a bit higher in pitch than it was moments ago. When I nod, she shakes her head. "Unbelievable," she mutters. "No. I did *not* sleep with Russ. Although, not for his lack of trying. I only ever liked him as a friend, and after finding out what happened at the ranch, I told him off. I called him and told him I never want to hear from him again before I went to the bar."

"*That's* who you were on the phone with?" I ask, dropping the taco I'm holding.

She smirks and teasingly says, "You really stalked me while I was on your ranch, didn't you?"

"I was coming with dinner, and I could hear you through the door. You were loud. I thought it was a boyfriend you were breaking up with or something."

She shakes her head, her smile replaced by a somber look. "I haven't had a boyfriend in a few years. I haven't had time."

"I'm sorry," I mumble.

The conversation lulls, and the two of us enjoy our food in silence. She keeps scrunching her eyebrows and relaxing them. I have a feeling she wants to ask me more questions but is unsure how. In all honesty, I'm not sure I'd be ready to answer her questions, so I let the silence stretch between us.

She yawns, and I look at my watch. It's getting late. I pay the bill, after refusing to let her help, and we get up to leave. The restaurant is close to her apartment, so we walk back. We still haven't breached the topic of where exactly I'm sleeping.

She unlocks the door to the building and holds it open for me. She stops and turns to me as she enters the hallway. "How did you get in the building, anyway?"

I smirk a cocky grin at her. "Hit every button outside until someone let me in."

"Great. Good to know my neighbors will let just anyone into the building because they are annoyed with a buzzer." She rolls her eyes but smiles. *God, her smile is something else.* Her whole face lights up. I've missed it so damn much. "Do you have any luggage with you?"

I was in such a rush to get a flight; I didn't even think of packing anything. I threw clothes on and pushed Holden out of my place to drive to the airport. Then, I spent way too much money on a last-minute flight so I could get here. Clothes were the last thing on my mind.

I rub the back of my neck and offer her a shy smile. "I was more concerned with getting here today than with packing clothes. I can sleep in this and pick a few things up tomorrow."

We reach her floor, and she pushes the front door open. I walk in behind her, locking the door. The air around us shifts. It's charged, heated. She must feel it, too, because she shifts her weight and looks around the room. I take a step closer, and her scent surrounds me. God, to have this girl in my arms would feel like heaven. "Where would you like me to sleep for the night?" My voice is low and a little raspy with need.

She licks her lips and swallows hard, popping her mouth open in surprise. She takes a small step back. The urge to stalk her, invade her space is strong, and I have to force myself to keep my feet planted. "How about you sleep on the couch?"

I didn't expect her to let me sleep in bed with her. I know I haven't earned that yet, but I was hopeful. Whatever she wants, though, I'm willing to give her. She hurries to her room, taking the heat and desire with her. She comes back with an extra blanket, pillow, and a sheet to cover the couch, and I help her set up my make-shift bed.

She tells me how she needs to go into the office early, but she will give me a key so I can get in and out without a problem. I have no idea what I'm going to do for the day, but I don't want to overstay my welcome.

"How long are you planning on staying?" she asks as she spreads out the blanket.

"I'm not sure. I haven't really planned things out yet. I guess that all depends on how long you want me to stay."

I feel like I'm in high school all over again, a bundle of nerves as I wait on bated breath for her reply.

"Oh. I-I don't know," she stumbles. "I didn't expect you to come here." She looks down and twists her fingers together. "Honestly, I figured I really would never see you again, so this is completely unexpected. What about the ranch?"

I think about it for a minute before I answer. Mom, Dad, and Holden can hold the fort down for a few days. "They'll be fine for a few days. I'd love to see Boston. I've never been here. Maybe you can show me some of the sights?"

She smiles wide and nods. "Sure. I can ask my boss about taking a few days off. Let her know something unexpected has come up and that I need time."

I shake my head. "I don't want to put you out like that. You have work. Go in, and if she says to take the time off, then fine. Otherwise, I can see some of the city myself, or I can wait for you to come home. Maybe I can pop into the office and see you. Pick you up for lunch or something?"

Her eyes light up as I finish. "Yeah. I'd like that a lot. Maybe we can show you the blueprints for the cabins along with the mock-up. It will be ready in a day or so."

"Sounds like a date."

She yawns and covers her mouth with the back of her hand. "Sorry, I was up early this morning for my flight. I'm beat."

I place my hands on her upper arms, and the heat of her body works its way down through my own, settling deep in my gut. I place a chaste kiss to her warm cheek. "Have a good night, Lana. We'll talk in the morning."

She shows me how to use the television before she walks down the hallway to her room and closes the door behind her. I should be tired, but I'm not. Not when I know she's so close to me. Not when everything in her apartment smells like her, and I have been semi-hard since she let me in here earlier today.

I kick my boots off and push my pants down, pulling them off one leg at a time. I then pull my shirt over my head and sit on the couch. I take my phone out, calling Holden, and he answers right before it goes to voicemail.

"Hey, man, did she forgive you? You getting laid yet?" he jokes. It's good to hear him happy, unlike this morning.

"Yeah, things seem pretty good between us. She's letting me crash on her couch tonight. I'm going to have to get some clothes tomorrow, though. I really didn't think this through, huh?" I keep my voice down; I don't want Lana to know I'm talking about her. "She told Russ to basically fuck off."

"Yeah? When?" Surprise is evident in his voice.

"The night she went to the bar. She told me about it tonight. We had a nice talk over dinner."

"And now she's cockblocking you by making you sleep on the couch?"

"No. This is better, anyway. I want to take things slow with her. I don't want to fuck this up when I have a chance to make things right. I just don't know what we're going to do. Her family and career are here, and mine is back home. I couldn't ask her to move her life just for me. I think I need to spend the week getting to know her."

"A week?" Holden yells into the phone. I pull it away from my ear to avoid my eardrum rupturing.

"Yeah. You, Mom, and Dad can hold everything down. We have a light group this week. Please, Holden. I need to find out if this thing between us could work. I need to know I tried. I don't want to regret it for the rest of my life."

He laughs. "Man, she's got you whipped already, and you haven't even been there for twenty-four hours."

"I'm not whipped, but I'm falling hard for her again."

CHAPTER 11

LANA

I've been tossing and turning for the better part of an hour. I *was* tired when I left Tristan in my living room. As soon as I closed my bedroom door, I became very aware of him in my apartment. I want nothing more than to feel his strong arms wrapped around me, holding me, caressing me. If I'm being honest with myself, it's been too long since I've gotten off, and knowing Tristan would be willing and is in the other room has my body wired.

I finally kick the covers off me and lie on my back, staring at the ceiling. I listen to the cars below me and the T, off in the distance. The rattling cars took some getting used to. I huff and get up, quietly opening my door. The living room is dark, so I tip-toe down the hall as to not wake him.

"Lana, what are you doing?" he asks.

Even in the dim light of the living room, I can make out his perfect body. He's lying on top of the blanket, his arm under his head and one leg bent at the knee.

"I was having a hard time sleeping and thought I'd check on you."

"Yeah, I can't sleep either. There's a lot of noise out here. How'd you get used to it?"

I shrug, and I know he can see me. The moonlight is casting a soft hue over my body. "Had to, I suppose. It is a bit quieter in my room. If you want, you can sleep in there—with me." *Oh God, I can't believe I just offered him my bed.* Wasn't the reason I banished him to the couch because I didn't think I'd be able to handle being in bed with him without us having sex?

He sits up and smirks. "Only if you're sure. I don't want you to feel you have to do anything you don't want to do."

"Yeah, I think we will both sleep better that way. You know, as far as comfort goes. I have a long day of work tomorrow, too," I try to rationalize. Who am I kidding, though? I want to push him down onto the bed and sink down on him, taking everything he will give me.

He stands in front of me, wearing nothing but dark boxer briefs. I can see out the bulge in the front, and I clench my thighs, hoping to ward off my impending need. I slowly raise my eyes, taking in every curve and crevice of his chiseled body. Even in the soft light of the room, I can make out the lines of his abs.

Seriously, how does one get that jacked? There's no way it's from working the ranch alone. He clasps his hands in front of him, hiding himself, and smirks when I lick my lips.

"You sure sharing a bed is going to be for the best?"

I nod slowly and close my eyes to rid the dirty thoughts from my mind. "Yes, hopefully, we can both get some sleep."

He follows me down the hall, and I climb back into my side as he climbs into the other, pulling the blankets up to his waist. I have a full-sized bed, and with the width of his shoulders, I feel like we're right on top of one another. I turn, giving him my back, and snuggle down, trying to get comfortable.

"Night, Tristan."

"Goodnight, Lana," he whispers.

Talk about vivid dreams. I'm surprised I didn't wake up to an orgasm with the way my mind was running rampant. When I finally pull myself from my amazingly delicious dreams, Tristan has his arm draped over my waist, my butt snug against his hard length. His breathing is deep and even, so I don't want to wake him, but I need to get out of his grasp before I do something I regret. *Although, I might not if it plays out the way it did in my mind.*

I wiggle my way out from under his arm, finish my morning business, and head into the kitchen to make coffee. I normally don't eat a lot of breakfast, but I can't leave him to fend for himself. I pull a carton of eggs out, some bread, butter, and bacon. It's a good thing I was craving bacon when I passed by it in the grocery store yesterday.

I turn on the coffee maker and make a cup as the bacon sizzles in the pan. I hear the sink in the bathroom running and know he's awake. I check myself quickly in my phone's reflection before he rounds the corner into view. He has his jeans on but has left them unbuttoned, and his shirt is still absent.

Holy. Shit. In the light, he's even more delectable than he was last night. My lady bits are doing a happy dance, hoping to get lucky, and I shut that shit down real fast.

"How'd you sleep?" I ask, turning the bacon over. I hold a mug up to him, and he nods at my silent question. Coffee is a must this early.

"Better once I moved to the bedroom. You're right; it is a lot quieter than the living room." He lifts the mug to his lips and takes a sip of the steaming liquid.

"Have a seat. Breakfast will be ready soon."

"Can I help?" He motions to the frying pan with the crackling bacon.

"Sure. Want to pop the toast in? I'll have the eggs done in a few minutes. How do you like them cooked?"

The two of us dance around one another in my small kitchen. The scary thing about this whole situation is it feels so natural, him being here. We talk and eat, sharing stories and adventures before I finally have to get ready for work.

I take a fast shower and get ready in fifteen minutes flat. When I come back out, Tristan is sitting on the couch, flipping through television channels. He stops when he sees me and lets out a low whistle. Talk about a boost to a girl's ego. I smile bashfully and bat my hand in front of me. I hand him an extra key and give him my cell phone number to get in touch with me if he needs to.

"I should be home by five-thirty. If something comes up, please call or text me. There are tons of stores around, so go check some out to get some clothes. Is there anything else you need before I go?" I ask, mentally running through all the things I want to do to him.

He stands, wraps one hand over my hip, and pulls me flush with his body. When he hovers his mouth inches from mine, I whimper. His breath fans over my face, and I think I'm going to burst when he closes the distance and his lips touch mine. Electricity runs from my lips to my toes. Where his hand rests on me feels like an inferno. I wrap my arms around his neck, pulling him further into the kiss—deepening it.

I can stay home, right? They don't need me. He walks me backward and presses me against the wall, pinning me beneath his weight. My nipples harden under my clothing, and I rock my core against him, feeling how hard he is for me. I hike my leg over his hip, and he grabs it, rocking harder into me. I moan into the kiss as he deepens it, taking what he needs.

He rubs his hard length against me one more time before breaking the kiss. My face is flushed, and I'm sure my hair is sticking up in spots, the frizz never fully dying down. I keep my eyes closed another second to catch my breath before I open them. His eyes are dark and lust-blown, his breathing matching my own. I clutch his shirt in my tiny fists and try to pull him back for more. When he drops my leg, I know that's it for now.

He clears his throat, but it does nothing to ease the ache between my legs. "Don't want to get you in trouble," he says, his voice husky with need.

"I could be a little late," I say, hoping he'll change his mind and fuck me senseless. It's been too long since I've gotten any, and with him, I *know* it would be good.

He laughs and shakes his head, then lowers his forehead to mine. "You're gonna be the death of me. Go so you can get back. I'll make dinner tonight."

My smile widens, and my eyes light up. "You're going to make me dinner?" A hint of disbelief is laced in my words.

He mocks offense and covers his heart with his hand. "I'll have you know, I'm a great cook. Wait 'til tonight. You're in for a treat."

I nod and turn to go. He gives my butt a little slap, and I jump, glancing over my shoulder at him with a smirk. I wave bye and leave to get to work. If I go straight there, I should only be about ten minutes late. I'm dragging my feet, though, and work is the last place I want to be. I'd rather see a baseball game with Tristan. *Are the Red Sox even playing tonight?* I'm not an avid watcher, but I've been to a few games. They are pretty fun to watch live, especially when the team is winning. The crowd is infectious.

I pull out my phone to call Bethany. She's never going to believe all this. I'd filled her in on everything when I got to Wyoming, but haven't had a chance to give her updates on anything else. We were supposed to talk last night, but with Tristan showing up unexpectedly, that didn't happen. Her cheery voice fills the line.

"Weren't we supposed to talk last night? What happened?"

"He's here."

"Who's there?"

"Tristan. He was sitting outside my apartment last night. We spent a fair amount of the night talking, and he apologized for everything. For what happened ten years ago, for not saying bye to me before I left." I slow my walking, so she doesn't hear how winded I'm getting from the brisk pace. *Note to self: do more cardio.*

"You've got to be shitting me. Did you forgive him?" I smile, thinking of our make-out session minutes earlier. "Oh my God! You slept with him, didn't you?" Her voice comes through so loud, the man next to me glances at me and smirks.

"No, Beth. We didn't sleep together. I'm not sure what to do about this. He said he wants to try to make things work between us, but I just don't know. We live in different parts of the country. Long-distance is never a good thing. It's hard." I bite my thumbnail as I stop outside my building doors so I can finish the conversation.

"Do you think he's worth it?"

Do I? I mean, I know how I feel when I'm with him. I know how my body reacts and how my mind wanders. I know I want a chance to see what happens, so I don't have to wonder what if. "I think I want to try."

"There you go, then. See what happens." She takes a deep breath. "Plus, you owe me some crazy sex stories. I need to live through your dating life!"

I feel my face heat up as she continues to laugh. I give her a quick goodbye and walk into my office to start my day. I hope it goes by fast.

Home. Finally, I'm home. I have never been so excited to walk through my front door as I am right this minute. I smell something delicious the moment I step foot on my floor, and one of my neighbors must have smelled it, too, because she's poking her head out. She makes a comment about hiring a chef, and I laugh it off, telling her it's a friend.

Friend. That's what he is, right? Maybe a friend with benefits? If I can ever get that far with him. Seems like he keeps putting the brakes on things. That's a fact I shouldn't actually be upset about. He's trying to do this the right way, not just diving into the deep end. I have to admire his strength.

I turn the knob, and the front door opens with ease. Spices and sweetness fill my senses, and I start to drool. I have no idea what he's making, but it sure smells amazing. His back is still to me as I take in his broad shoulders, slim waist, and jean-clad legs. This man is sex, walking. He makes me want to strip naked and say, "Take me, I'm yours."

I drop my keys on the counter, and he turns to face me, a boyish grin on his handsome face. He pushes some stray hair out of his eyes as he looks at me from head to toe. "Damn," he says quietly.

"What's that amazing smell? The woman across the hall wants some." He turns back to the stove and stirs the pot. I put my purse down and stroll up to him, wrapping my arms around his waist, laying my head on his back. I kiss the spot where my cheek was resting, and he hums his appreciation.

"Barbeque chicken, baked beans, and mashed potatoes. Hope you're hungry." He turns in my grasp and pulls me to him for a full-frontal hug, kissing the top of my head.

"Wow, mister. I really didn't think you were serious about

being able to cook. I'm impressed." I pull away from him. "I'm going to change. I'll be back in a few minutes."

I rush to my bedroom to get into pajamas for the night. As I strip out of the clothes I wore today, I look at the bra and panties I have on. They're comfortable, but they don't scream sexy. They aren't even matching. I shimmy out of them and decide to go braless, but I pull on a pair of lacy red undies. They were my favorite pair when I bought them a few months ago, but I haven't had a reason to wear them besides to feel better about myself.

I pull on my tank top and shorts and slip out of my room. Tristan opened a bottle of wine, and there are two glasses sitting on the table. I grab a glass, taking a small sip. He's working on plating food, and I smile at the scene in front of me. It's so domestic and personal. Not many men cook like this. Sure, they can make burgers and pizza, but this took a lot of work and a lot of groceries. I know for a fact I didn't have any of this stuff in my fridge or pantry.

Those guys I just mentioned—that's me. I know how to cook, and I can cook a lot of stuff, but I usually don't have time.

"How much did this cost you?" I ask, taking a seat as he places a plate in front of me.

He shrugs. "Doesn't matter. I wanted to do something nice for you. Tell me about your day."

Well, I spent my entire day thinking about you and your sexy as sin body, and I watched the clock like a hawk. I thought the day was never going to end. I don't want to push him, though. "It was fine. Blueprints are almost done for the cabins if you want to come in tomorrow to see them. I can tell Eloise you are going to come by."

I take a bite of the beans and close my eyes for a moment, letting the sweet heat melt on my tongue. Oh God, this tastes so good. Next, I take a bite of the potatoes, and same thing. *Seriously, how can this be that good?*

He smirks as he watches me eat and finally answers. "Yeah, I'd love to come by and see where you work. I was able to get some clothes and also a bag to get everything home. I made sure to get at least one pair of nice pants and a button-down in case I was able to go in."

"I'll text her after dinner to let her know you'll be by."

"How are you going to explain me being in Massachusetts?" He takes a bite of chicken, and some barbecue sauce is left on his cheek. I reach my thumb out and swipe it away, sucking the sweet sauce into my mouth. He groans and shifts in his seat. I bite my lip and decide that maybe I can entice him by teasing him.

I swipe my finger through some sauce on my own chicken and push it toward his mouth. I rub the sauce over his lips until he opens and sucks it clean.

"You're going to be the death of me, woman."

"Then, maybe you and I will die happy."

CHAPTER 12

TRISTAN

J'm painfully hard throughout the rest of dinner. Lana keeps making those sexy moaning noises and batting her eyes at me, trying to act innocent. *I see right through that, babe.* She helps clean the dishes and put everything away.

She walks down the hall toward her bedroom, adding an extra sway to her hips as she goes. I can't take it anymore—the animal within me has broken through. I grab her arm, spin her around, and press her against the wall with such force her back bounces a little. I wrap one arm around her waist, pulling her lower body to me, place my other hand around the back of her neck, and press my lips to hers forcefully.

"Open," I demand, and she does, allowing me to slide my tongue into her mouth, deepening the kiss. She melts into my embrace, and I push my weight into her, keeping her standing. Her nipples pebble under that thin shirt, and I pull back just long enough to rip it over her head.

Her chest heaves as I take in my fill of her perfect breasts. "Beautiful," I murmur before kissing a path down her neck.

She tilts her head, giving me room, and rakes her fingers

through my locks, adding an extra tug. I hiss, but it only fuels me on, makes me want her more than should be possible. I take one of her nipples into my mouth, and she gasps as I tug with my teeth before soothing the sting with my tongue. She reaches between us, trying to find my cock. I'm afraid if she plays with it, I'll come in my pants. I'm wound too tight.

Instead, I stand tall and grasp her behind her legs, pulling her onto my waist so I can carry her into the bedroom. I toss her down, and she giggles and tries to crawl up the bed. I shake my head at her and pull her ankles so they dangle over the edge. I grip her shorts, slowly easing them down her legs, teasing her with soft touches as I go. *I want her soaked before I taste her.* I almost come at the sight of the most sinful panties I've ever seen.

Red. Fucking. Lace.

I groan and shift myself in my pants before I go to work. She bites her lip and smirks as I watch her from my spot on the floor. I run my fingers up and down her legs, adding kisses here and there. Then, I trace the edges of her panties, making goosebumps rise in my wake. She moans and closes her eyes, lost in the sensations, lost in me.

I climb up on the bed, kissing her everywhere except where I know she wants it the most. She pushes her fingers into my hair and tries to put my face where she wants it, but I unwrap her hands and press them above her head.

"You're going to keep your hands there, or I'll stop," I warn.

"Oh, God, please, Tristan. Stop torturing me," she mewls and bucks her hips up.

I chuckle, dark and full of dirty promises. "You'll get what I give you when I'm ready. Keep begging, though. I like it."

I nip the inside of her thigh, and she presses her hips up to me again. I kiss her stomach, right about the panty-line, and stick my tongue out to lick her belly button. She sucks her stomach in on an inhale and releases a shaky breath. I finally put her out of her misery and plant a kiss on top of her mound. Her panties are soaked, and I take a deep breath, savoring how she smells.

I hook my fingers around her panties and pull them down her legs, flinging them into the corner somewhere.

"Can I touch you, please?" she asks.

I glance up, and her arms are exactly where I've left them. Good girls who listen get rewarded, and I'm about to feast until she comes apart under me. Then, I want to fuck her until we both can't take it anymore. I nod, and she digs her nails into my hair, the same time my tongue peeks out to taste her for the first time in a decade.

This. This is heaven. Between her legs is the only place I want to be.

"Oh, Tristan," she moans as I find all the secret spots that turn her to mush. I lick her with expertise, and when my fingers slip into her, I almost come. She squeezes them so tight as she fights to keep her own orgasm at bay.

"Baby, let go. Come for me," I urge.

After another few stokes and a few more perfectly timed licks, she arches her back and pulls me closer as she comes all over me. I continue to lap up everything she gives, and when her body relaxes, I stand up. Her eyes are glued to the bulge in my pants. She flips around and crawls to the edge, her fingers moving deftly, quickly undoing my button and zipper. She tugs on my pants, and I help her pull them down my legs before pulling my shirt over my head.

Her eyes are dark, full of lust, and when she takes my length into her hand, I know that's it. I don't want another girl to touch me ever again. My entire body hums under her touch like it remembers how perfect she was so long ago. She leans forward and sucks the tip into her mouth. I close my eyes and drop my head back, unable to hold back the moan. She swirls her tongue over the head and sucks me further into her mouth

"Lana, you can't. I-I'm not going to last," I manage to push out.

I feel the beginning stages of my orgasm low in my spine, so I pull her off me with a pop. I brush some stray hair out of her eyes and smile at her, then kiss the tip of her nose, and she scrunches her face as my stubble tickles her.

"I want to be inside you when I come. I'm not going to last, though," I warn.

She nods, and I pull a condom out of my pants pocket on the floor. I rip the foil and roll it on. When I climb on the bed, she lays back, spreading her legs to give me room to crawl between them. She glistens from her earlier orgasm, and I can't wait to feel her warmth envelop me. She reaches between up and helps guide me to her entrance.

I slowly thrust my hips forward, and her eyes roll back as I push all the way in, settling myself deep within her. I drop my forehead, savoring the feeling of being inside her again. She feels even better than I remember, softer somehow. I want to stay here forever, encased in her.

"Tristan, please move," she says, pulling me from my thoughts.

I don't want this to end, but I know I'm only good for a few thrusts. I want to feel her come around me. It was a tease, having her come on my fingers. I find her engorged clit with the pad of my thumb and press down, making small circles as I sit back on my heels to watch myself slide in and out of her. She circles her hips and presses her fingers down over mine, helping me move over the nub how she likes it best.

I keep my thrusts slow as I build her up, her breathy moans and pants urging me to help her find her release.

"Lana, I'm going to come, baby. Are you there?" I clench

my teeth, trying to hold off. She doesn't even have to tell me. Her body goes rigid, and she clamps around me so tight it forces my own orgasm from me. I pound into her, giving her everything, making her take it as I extend both our pleasures.

I drop to my forearms, and she takes my face between her hands, kissing every part of it she can. I try to bring my heart rate down and breathe normally, but I still kiss her deeply when her lips find mine. I pull away after a few minutes to discard the condom and get us cleaned up.

That was amazing. *She* was amazing. She turns on her side, leaving her clothes on the floor, and I pull her against me. I kiss her head, and she mumbles something I can't quite make out. "Sleep, baby," I say before getting comfortable and falling asleep.

We didn't get to talk this morning, too busy kissing and bringing one another to another amazing orgasm. Then she was running late. She gave me her work address so I can show up today for an eleven o'clock appointment with her and Eloise to look over the blueprints and see the model they have constructed.

I stand outside the tall building and look at all the glass, shining in the sun like thousands of diamonds. The building is huge. I take the elevator up to the fifteenth floor, and when the doors open, I'm standing in front of a desk with a huge sign for *Smith and Quill Designs* behind the girl.

She smiles at me. "Hi, can I help you?"

"I have an appointment with Lana Robinson and Eloise Quill. My name is Tristan Ellis." I smile back at her. Her eyes light up, and she blushes a little before looking back at her screen.

"Great, I see you here. Please, have a seat, and Ms. Robinson will be out to get you in a few minutes. Can I offer you any water or coffee?"

I shake my head and take a seat. My leg is bouncing with energy. I need to see Lana. I haven't felt right since she left me alone this morning. After a few minutes, I feel her before I even see her. I turn in time to see Lana step into view, her smile sending waves of pleasure coursing through me.

"Mr. Ellis. So nice to see you again." I stand, and she extends her hand to me, keeping it professional between us. When I grasp her hand, her face reddens a little, and she looks to the ground. She's probably remembering where my fingers were this morning. *I want to be there again.*

"Nice to see you again as well."

"Please, follow me. Eloise Quill is already in the meeting room waiting for us."

We walk down the hall, and she checks to see if anyone is looking before giving me an unexpected peck on the lips. It's nothing more than a tease, and I want to pull her to me and demand more. But she's at work, and I don't want to get her in trouble, so she will have to make it up to me tonight.

I smirk and ask quietly, "What was that for?"

"I've missed you, and you look incredibly sexy in that button-down shirt," she whispers just loud enough for me to hear.

She doesn't give me time to say anything back before she knocks on the meeting room door and pushes it open. The space is large and bright with the curtains pulled back, showing off some of the Boston skyline.

Eloise stands and walks over to me, extending her hand for me to take. "Mr. Ellis, it's a pleasure to finally meet you."

We shake, and I extend the same greeting. I take a seat opposite of Lana, and we get started. She goes over the sample of the cabins and reviews the blueprints with me. I ask a few questions, and she answers them with ease. Eloise tosses in her two cents here and there, but mainly, she lets Lana control the meeting. It's amazing to watch her. She's definitely in her element here.

We wrap up about an hour later, and Lana walks me to the door. "Meet me downstairs. We'll go for lunch," she requests quietly.

I nod and fight the urge to kiss her on the cheek, instead giving her a firm handshake and adding a little extra squeeze for good measure. "See you in a few."

CHAPTER 13

LANA

*T*hat meeting went better than I expected. Eloise was smitten with Tristan, and who wouldn't be? He knows how to lay it on thick when he needs to. I reach my office and grab my purse, ready to get something to eat.

"He seems nice," Eloise says, standing in my doorway.

I look at her and smile. "Yes, he is. It was a pleasure getting to work with him."

She smirks. "He wouldn't be the history that was at *Black Stallion Ranch*, would he?"

I blush and try to dodge the question. "I'm glad you got to meet him. He seems happy with the work we've done."

"Lana, sit for a minute." She closes my door, takes a seat opposite my desk, and crosses her shapely legs. I smooth my skirt under my butt and sit at the edge, nervous energy pooling in my stomach. "He didn't fly all the way over here for a meeting. I'm glad I had the opportunity to meet him, he seems like a nice man, but I want to make sure things are okay with you. A few days ago, you wanted to give this account to someone else.

Now, if I heard you in the meeting correct, you want to go back out to spearhead the construction?"

I furrow my brows, confused as to what she's getting at. "Yes. Normally, we send someone out during the initial construction for a few weeks, and then again toward the end to make sure everything is running smoothly. I did the work, so I feel I should go out and supervise. Is there a problem?"

She shakes her head. "I don't want to see you get hurt. You know I think very highly of you. You are an extremely hard worker. You have done a lot for this company, and I appreciate that. He's a nice boy and seems to have a good head on his shoulders, just be careful."

My expression softens. I did share a fair amount when I told her I shouldn't be working the account, and I can see where she's coming from. "Thank you, Eloise. I'll be fine."

"Good. Also, I got a call this morning from a Simone Carrington from London, England." I tense at the mention of her name. "She told me you two met in Wyoming, and she wants to hire you to do some redesign work. Seems you have a lot of fans there."

I smile weakly. "Yeah, I know her family. We met the first time I went to the ranch. She mentioned wanting to hire someone for design work, and I gave her the information for *Quill and Smith Designs*." I take a deep breath, hoping to ease the thrumming of my heartbeat in my ears. "I can't take that account. You have to send someone else."

She shakes her head as her smile fades. "She specifically said she wanted you to do the designs." I lean back in my seat and push out a breath. "Go to lunch with Tristan, and we will figure it out when you get back."

I bite back a smile as she leaves my office, then I scurry down to meet the man who makes my heart beat a little faster.

I've been trying to figure out how I'm going to tell Tristan about my upcoming trip without him flying off the deep end. I know his thoughts on Russ, and if I'm being honest, I share some of those opinions. This isn't about Russ, though; this is about Simone. She did mention wanting me to do some designs when I saw her last week, but I didn't think she was serious.

I stand outside my front door, trying to find the courage to face him and tell him, but I'm chicken shit. I think it might be best for me to not mention who I am going to be helping. Client confidentiality and all that, right? *Is that even a thing in my line of work?*

When I push open my door, he sure is a sight for sore eyes. He's lounging on my couch in a t-shirt and basketball shorts. I let my eyes wander for just a minute, getting my fill of him. *Damn, I am one lucky woman.* He smiles and closes the gap between us, wrapping me up in his arms and planting a kiss on my lips.

"I could get used to coming home like this every night." I sigh as he kisses my neck.

"You look good enough to eat. Watching you take control of that meeting today was something else." He nips my earlobe, and a pang of need hits me hard in my center.

"You already told me that today." I swat his arm, trying to pull from his grasp.

"You need a reminder." He swats my ass with his large hand as I moan. "This skirt drove me crazy today. Whoever designed it needs a standing ovation. I kept fantasizing about bending you over the table in the meeting and having my way with you."

"Oh, God." I close my eyes, picturing it. Picturing the thrill of being in my office as we do something so dirty where we could get caught.

He pushes me backward until we are next to the couch and then spins me around, pressing me down so my hands are on the armrest. I widen my stance, knowing exactly what he wants. He's about to get the surprise of a lifetime when he sees I'm not wearing any panties.

He pushes my skirt over my hips and groans. "Are you kidding me? You haven't been wearing any all day?"

I look over my shoulder and shake my head, a smile creeping up. He drags his fingers through my soaked folds, then brings them to his mouth for a taste. I bite my lip; the scene is so erotic. I want him in me so bad. I want to feel all of him, no barrier.

"Tristan?"

"Yeah, babe?" he asks, rubbing himself against my ass.

"I want to feel all of you. No condom." I hold my breath, waiting for his answer.

I feel his dick pulse against me, so I know I didn't scare him too bad. He steps back long enough to pull his shorts down and slicks himself up with my arousal. When he pushes the tip in, I think I've died and gone to heaven. He inches in slowly, each of us moaning with the pure ecstasy of this moment. I'm wound so tight from just thinking about having him in me that it's only a few thrusts before I come apart on him, thrusting my hips back to extend my own euphoria.

He grips tight on my hips, and I'm sure I'll have bruises in the morning, but I don't care. He comes quickly, grunting and breathing heavily as he empties everything into me. He slowly pulls out and places his hand on my back to keep me in place. He hurries to the bathroom to get a cloth and helps clean both of us up, like the gentleman he is.

When I turn to face him, I'm smiling so bright I'm

surprised my face hasn't cracked. I expected his expression to match mine, but there are worry lines marring his perfect face. I somber up quickly.

"What's wrong?"

He drags his hands down his face and then pushes his fingers through his hair. "You're the only one I've ever had that way. Ten years ago, when I took you that way, that was the first and last time until now."

I hold his face in my hands. "You're the only one I've ever had sex with that way, too."

His eyes light up. "Really?"

I shrug and kick off my heels, making me almost a foot shorter than him. "Yeah. When you took my virginity, I wanted to have that first experience with you, and no one has ever been good enough to have it with again."

He's rendered speechless, and I stand on my tip-toes to kiss him. Everything seems right between us until I remember the reason I didn't want to come home. I need to tell him about my upcoming trip. Hillary booked my flight to London for tomorrow night, returning Saturday morning.

I put off telling him and decide to order some food and watch a movie snuggled on the couch. I'm not ready to let him go just yet. I want to stay in our bubble just a bit longer. That all comes to a halt when his phone rings, and his dad's name flashes across the screen.

"Dad, what's wrong?" He sits forward, resting his elbows on his knees.

The volume on his phone is just loud enough for me to hear some of what he says. *Mom has been in an accident. Not her fault. Drunk driver.* Everything changes in an instant. The electric energy fizzles and turns dark. Now, my goosebumps aren't because of his touch—it's fear.

He stands and walks to the bedroom, leaving me sitting

there alone to wonder. I want to give him space, but I struggle because I want to hold him and take away some of the pain I know he must be feeling. So, I do the next best thing. I pull open my computer and start looking for the next flight to Laramie.

I find a flight that leaves tomorrow morning at six and start typing in all of his information. He walks back into the room, looking panicked. His eyes are wide, and he can't focus on any one thing in the room.

"I found you a flight for six tomorrow morning. It's the first one with availability."

He nods. "Okay, thanks," he mumbles as I finish typing in my credit card information.

Last-minute flight, eight hundred dollars for one way. I know he probably paid more than that to come out here, and honestly, I wouldn't bat an eye if it meant helping him get to his family. His mom has always been so loving and welcoming to me. Even after all this time.

"Do you want to talk about it?" I urge, keeping my voice quiet.

"No." He rubs his forehead and closes his eyes. "I have a headache and an early morning. I think I'm going to pack my stuff and go to bed."

"Okay. I'll help," I offer.

"No. It's fine. I can do it on my own."

Please, don't shut me out, Tristan. I don't say that, though. "Okay," falls from my lips as I watch him walk away.

After some time has passed, I turn the light off in the living room and tip-toe into the bedroom. All the lights are off, and his back is to the door. His breathing seems deep and even, and I wonder how he can even sleep. I pull the covers down and crawl under them, kissing his shoulder before I turn my back to him.

He shifts, pulls me into his arms, and kisses the back of my head. "I'm sorry. It's a lot to deal with right now, and I do better alone."

"I know. I don't want to push you, but I don't want you to shut me out either. I'm here to talk when you're ready," I say quietly.

"Thank you, Lana. You mean the world to me. Please, don't give up on me. I'll come around."

"I know. I'll be waiting."

CHAPTER 14

TRISTAN

*T*his damn flight feels like it's taking days, not hours.
There is still another hour until we land, and I
haven't gotten any more updates from Dad. They put her in a
medically induced coma due to brain swelling. He told me she
has a bunch of broken bones, and the doctor was surprised
she'd made it through.

My leg bounces with nervous energy as I replay the conversation in my head. Holden is watching over things at the ranch
since Dad refuses to leave the hospital. I texted him last night to
tell him I'm coming home, and he told me everything is going to
work out. I pray to God he's right.

The stewardess walks past me and offers me something to
drink. Hard liquor would be great right now, but I need to keep
a clear head. I shake my head and close my eyes, trying to stop
the building headache.

Lana was so fucking sweet, doing this for me. I wish she
was able to come with me, though. I never realized how lost I
felt until she stepped foot in my life again. I can feel it when
she's not close, and I fucking hate it. I am finally starting to feel

like my life is turning around, and I have her to thank for it. I'm going out of my fucking mind without her here. When she came to bed last night, my racing mind finally settled.

I need that.

I need her.

She told me about an upcoming trip for a new client, so she will be out of the country for a few days. I didn't want to pry too much since it's her job, so I settled on getting a schedule when we could talk to catch up.

Finally, the captain makes an announcement about our initial descent into Laramie, and for the first time this entire trip, the knot in my chest loosens, and I feel I can breathe easier. I rub the spot of my chest that has been under pressure for too long and take a deep breath.

I'm too impatient, and since we are close to the ground, I take my phone off airplane mode and pull up a text to Holden.

Me: *I'm almost there. Any news from my dad?*

Holden: *Not yet, want me to come get you?*

Me: *No, I'm going right to the hospital to see Mom. Let me know if anything major happens, and I'll keep you posted.*

I place my phone to my ear, listening as it rings, and the woman next to me glares at me. *I really don't give a shit, lady.* It switches to voicemail, and I hang up without leaving a message. The wheels hit the tarmac, and we taxi up to the gate. If they don't let me off this flying tin can soon, I'm going to burst.

When they finally free me, I race to the exit, locating my ride easily. I give her the address for the hospital and pray she's a fast driver.

As I walk down the hallway to Mom's room, my heart feels

like it's beating out of my chest. My phone rings with a new message, and when I see who it is, a calm washes over me. Lana.

Lana: *I miss you. I hope everything is okay with your mom and the flight was good. Call me when you have a few minutes of free time.*

God, I want to call her so bad. She has no idea how perfect her timing is, but right now, it's important I get to Mom and get an update. I take a deep breath when I locate her room, and a nurse carrying a small tray closes the door tight behind her. I knock and push the door open. Dad looks up at me and offers a small smile in my direction.

"Hey, Dad. How is she?"

"Stable. They took her off the medicine keeping her in a coma, but she still hasn't woken up yet. Docs said they aren't worried. It can take a few days." He looks back at her, lifts her hand to his lips, and plants a gentle kiss on the back of it.

The guilt eats me alive as I look at her so helpless on the bed. Then I start to remember all the time she's spent here already. All the chemo appointments and the days she would lay in bed all day, too tired to move. Fear races up my spine at the thought of her not pulling through. I should have been home so she didn't have to drive. "I shouldn't have gone away. I should have been here for her. It wouldn't have happened if I was here," I berate myself.

"Tristan, this isn't your fault. You're not going to blame yourself for this." His voice leaves no room for discussion, and I know if I keep pushing, it will end in an argument.

He stands and stretches. "Take a little time with her. I'm going to get something to eat in the cafeteria. I'll be back soon. Call me if anything changes while I'm away." He places his hands on my strong shoulders, and I feel like a five-year-old boy again under the critical eye of my father. "I'm glad you went, son. There was something special between the two of you back then. You should get the chance to see if she's what you want." He pulls me into a hug and releases me just as fast.

I take his seat and take Mom's hand in mine. She feels so frail, so sick. Her skin feels as thin as paper under my calloused fingers.

"Hey, Mom. Not sure if you can hear me, but I went to see Lana."

I spend the next thirty or so minutes talking about what's been going on for the past three days. I tell her I surprised Lana and how she reacted differently than I thought she would. I also tell her how she forgave me and that we are going to find a way to make it work—everything I know she would want to know about.

The steady beeping of the machines is the only indicator that my mom is still here. I watch her constant heartbeat on the screen, hoping for any other indicator of her hearing or under-standing me. A few times, I thought I felt her squeeze my hand a little, but it could have been wishful thinking.

When Dad gets back, I ask him if he wants to go home for a bit, but he refuses to leave Mom. I decide it's best to leave them alone for a while and check on things at the ranch. I know he'll call me as soon as there's a change in her condition.

The car pulls up outside my house, and Holden is there waiting for me. I gave him some updates on the car ride over. I haven't called Lana yet, but I wanted to wait until I got home. Holden and I talk for a few minutes about some supplies that need to be ordered, and I tell him to get whatever he needs before I go upstairs to my old room and plop down on my bed to call Lana. She answers on the first ring.

"Tristan," she says on a breath.

"Hey, sorry I didn't call sooner. I got your text when I got to the hospital, but I wanted to see Mom first." I close my eyes and rub my forehead, a stress headache on its way.

"That's fine. I'm just glad to hear your voice. How is she?"

"She's okay. We're waiting for her to wake up from the coma. They took her off the medicine to keep her in that state, but she's not waking up yet."

"How long can that take?"

I shrug my shoulders, even though she can't see me. "Don't know. Hopefully, soon. Dad didn't want to leave, but I wanted to check on things here and call you."

"I'm glad you did. I miss you. I fly out tonight for England."

"England? That's where you're going?" *Interesting that the company would send her there.*

She hesitates before answering. "Yeah. I'm working on a project with Mr. and Mrs. Carrington. When I saw her at the ranch, she mentioned having me come out to do some interior design work. I didn't think she was serious, but I'm the only one she wants, and Eloise didn't want to lose this client."

Just. Fucking. Great. This is all a ploy set up by Russ to get her out there. I know it is. My jealousy rears its ugly head, and I grit my teeth to stop from yelling.

When I don't say anything, she continues. "I've already told him off. I don't want to see him, and if I do, I'll tell him to leave me alone. It's just a job."

I know she's right, and she has never given me a reason to not trust her. Even when I think back to ten years ago, I let my ego get in the way, and I lost her. I can't do that again. I take a deep breath and push it out slowly, counting backward to calm my inner beast.

"I know. I trust you."

She pushes out a deep breath. Even without seeing her, I

know that was the right thing to say to ease her mind. "Don't worry about me. Keep me updated with your mom. I have a feeling everything's going to be okay."

"Yeah. Will do. Talk to you later. Have a safe flight." *I love you.* It's too soon. I'd scare her away, but I've always been one to fall hard and fast. And this feels right. So damn right.

We hang up with the words on the tip of my tongue, and I don't know what to do with myself. I'm angry at Russ. That piece of shit is going to be that close to *my* girl. I don't want him thinking it's okay to try to make a move on her. She's not available.

Yes, she is. No one ever said we were exclusive. She knows we are together now, right? I fight against my better judgment and don't text or call her. I don't want it taken the wrong way. I don't want her to think I don't trust her. It's *him* I don't trust.

I can't lay up here forever. I've got a ranch to run and guests to take care of. I take a fast shower and get outside to help Holden with the guests. It's an easy day since the ranch isn't full this week—not that it ever is now—so at least I don't have to worry when my mind wanders to my mom and Lana.

I haven't heard from Dad all day, and it's now late afternoon. I don't think the hospital will let him sleep there overnight, but maybe it's a special case for Mom. So, when he pulls up around eight at night, I meet him on the porch steps. He looks worn out.

"How's Mom?" I ask, not able to contain myself.

He takes a deep breath and pushes it out. "No changes as of yet. The doctors really thought she would be awake by now, but they still said not to worry. You know your mom. Can't rush her to do anything she's not ready to do." He chuckles and shakes her head. "Doctors still think she'll make a full recovery."

"Sounds like Mom."

He hums in response, and we both go inside. "So, tell me about this unexpected trip to see Lana Robinson?"

CHAPTER 15

LANA

I want a shower and bed. Red-eye flights are the worst. I'm lucky that Eloise sprung for a first-class flight, so I was able to have a bed for a while, even if it was uncomfortable. I stand in front of the mirror in the bathroom, giving myself a once over to make sure I look presentable. *I'd better be able to find some good coffee around this place.* I drag my small bag behind me so I can locate some caffeine and a bagel or something.

When I make it down to the luggage area, I stop dead in my tracks. *Why?* Russ is standing there, waiting for me. The last man I ever wanted to see again is the one I'm stuck with. I glance at the time on my phone; it's eight in the morning here, which means it's really early still in Wyoming. I want to call Tristan and complain, but I know he's had a tough day and probably needs sleep.

Maybe I can sneak back up the stairs before he sees me. Our eyes lock, and Russ smiles wide before closing the gap between us.

"Lana, welcome to England. Mum and Dad are thrilled

you're doing the design. They said they met up with you at the ranch, and you said you'd be delighted to help." He tries to take my bag from me, but I hold on tight to it. He frowns and looks at me.

"I told you I never wanted to see you again and told you to never contact me. I didn't want to take this job because of our past, but my boss said they didn't want anyone else to do it." I lower my voice so no one overhears us. "I want to make one thing perfectly clear. I am here for your parents. Not. You. Stay out of my way these next few days, and we'll be just fine."

He smiles. "Whatever you say, Lana."

Why don't I believe a word coming out of his mouth? He takes my bag, and when I try to protest, he walks in front of me. I have to practically run in my heels to keep up with him. I won't give him the satisfaction of knowing that, though, so I huff behind him. My calves are killing me by the time we make it to his car. I climb into the passenger seat and wait for him to join me.

He slides in, starts his car, and we're off. He keeps the conversation moving, telling me all the things his mom wants replaced in the house as I try my best to ignore him. I remember visiting, and while I stayed at his flat, we did have dinner at his parents' house once. It was a massive house. I'm not even sure you could call it that. It was more like a mansion.

"Did you get the flowers I sent you?" He glances between me and the road.

I cross my arms over my chest and stare out the window. "I got them."

He smirks, and I want to smack it off his stupid face. "I really am sorry, Lana. It was childish of me. I was a stupid kid when I told him that. I didn't think he would believe me."

I finally turn to look at him, disbelief settling across my face.

"You didn't think he would believe you? What about all those years when your family would go back to the ranch, and you tortured him by talking about me? Or how about how you told him we slept together?" I almost yell. I need to rein in my emotions. *Breathe, girl.*

"I never told him we slept together. I used to give him updates because I thought he would want to know how you were doing. He also seemed so sad, and I thought I could cheer him up a bit. Never worked though. He used to ignore me or avoid me, sending his lackey to do his work."

"His name is Holden."

He waves his hand, dismissing my statement. "Whatever. He's always tried to make me look bad in your eyes. He tried anything to keep you away from me that week. I just wanted someone else to hang out with, and you were pretty." He smiles. "*Are* pretty. Listen, no hard feelings. Let's try to put this behind us and be friends again."

He pulls into the driveway of his parents' home, and we get out. Can I be friends with him? After my last trip, I basically stopped talking to him because he gave me the creeps. Besides that and the thing with Tristan, he was always a decent friend to me.

He gathers my belongings from his car, and Simone opens the door, waving at us from the house.

"Hi, Mrs. Carrington. It's nice to see you again," I say as I walk up the three steps into her home. She pulls me into a hug and holds me at arm's length, examining me.

"Lana, dear, I didn't know you were coming."

What. The. Fuck.

My smile fades, and my eyes widen as I stare at her. "I-I'm here because you wanted to redo your house. You hired my company and insisted *I* do the design. That's what my boss told me."

She shakes her head. "I told them I wanted to hire the company and for them to send whoever they had available."

I turn to look at Russ, who has the good grace to turn red and look at his shoes. Strike one against forgiving him.

"I'm thrilled it's you, dear. You'll do a wonderful job. Please, come in. Let's discuss what I want and what room I want you to redo," she says as she pulls me into the house and leads me around.

The house looks the same as it did when I visited last time. Nothing has changed except for a few pictures of the kids. Russ and Regina are grown in these ones. They are pictures of their graduations from college and even pictures of Regina with an unknown man, whom I assume is her boyfriend.

She talks about her vision for the house, and I dutifully take notes as Russ trails behind us, no doubt waiting for this chance to explain. I'm sure he had something to do with it. I was willing to move past what happened ten years ago. When I called him last time, I was pissed, but this is insane. Forcing me to take this project because he wanted to see me? That borders on stalkerish.

She lets me sit in the dining room to work on some ideas I have, and she wants me to show her something later today so we can fine-tune it. Russ comes and goes throughout the morning, and when lunchtime hits, I'm fading fast.

"Come on, you need some coffee, and Mum only buys the rubbish stuff. You also need some lunch; otherwise, you will never make it through the rest of your day."

No. What I need is for you to leave me alone so I can finish this and get back to Tristan. "No, thanks. I'll eat later. I want to get this done."

I haven't heard from him yet today, and I'm getting worried. I pull my phone out and send him a quick message.

Me: *Haven't heard from you. Hope your mom is doing okay.*
I miss you.

I lock my phone, and he snatches it from my grasp. I pop my mouth open in surprise and stand just as quickly, holding out my hand.

"Give me my phone, Russ," I chastise.

"Not until you take a break and have some lunch with me. My treat. I want to be able to talk to you."

I march toward him and stand on my tip-toes as he holds it high above my head and out of reach. I smack him in the chest when he doesn't lower his arm.

"You're giving me my phone back, now!" I toss my hands up in the air. "I don't have time for this. I want to finish these designs and head to my hotel for the night. I've barely slept, and I'm jet-lagged."

He quiets his voice. "All the more reason to get food in your system. I just want to have a meal with you. I'm not trying anything."

My phone buzzes, and he looks at the I.D. He makes a face and holds it out for me to take. I snatch it out of his hand and open the message from Tristan.

Tristan: *No news yet. She's still in a coma. I'm going over there in a little bit, so I'll keep you updated. Thanks for asking. I miss you, too.*

Me: *I'll call you when I'm at the hotel for the night. Boy, do I have a story for you...*

I place my phone in my purse, away from Russ's grabby hands, and sit back down to work on a few more sketches. He sits in the chair next to me and watches me work, staying perfectly silent. I don't know if it's the fact he's sitting here watching me, or that he's so silent while doing it, but I'm so irritated.

I huff and drop my pencil, fold my hands on my drawing, and glare at him. "If I go to lunch, will you leave me alone?"

He places his hand over his heart and smiles. "I promise."

Eight o'clock and it feels like two in the morning. I am so tired and so happy to be able to lie down and get some sleep. Lunch with Russ wasn't as bad as I thought it would be. He gave me a chance to rip him a new ass hole, and then he cleared the air between us. I still don't fully forgive him, but I'm willing to try to move past *some* of it.

I want to call Tristan and get an update on everything. He picks up just before it goes to voicemail, and I can hear people talking in the background.

"Hey, babe," he answers, sounding happy.

"Hey. You sound happy. Good news, I hope?" I stifle a yawn as I listen to him speak.

"Yeah, Mom woke up this afternoon. She seems to be on the mend, but she has a lot of broken bones and won't be back up and running for another few months." I can hear his smile and relief over the phone.

"Tristan, that's great news. I'm so happy she's going to be okay."

"Me too. So, you have a story you want to share with me?"

"Boy do I ever."

I change into my pajamas as I tell him all about how Russ called my office, stating Simone only wanted me to take the account. Simone didn't even know about it and was just as

surprised as I was when I showed up at her house. I go on to tell
him about how Russ apologized for his behavior as well.

"*That's* what he told you?" He scoffs. "God, he's so full of
shit, Lana. He was doing more than giving me updates out of
the goodness of his heart. He did it to torture me. And he said
you were great. Who says that unless they mean in bed?"

Not that I think Russ is innocent, but this wouldn't be the
first time Tristan had it out for Russ. "You're making a big deal
out of this. Is it possible you misunderstood him? It wouldn't be
the first time you thought you heard something or saw something you didn't." I wince, knowing that cut deep, and his
silence confirms it. I sigh and rub my forehead. "I didn't call to
fight. I'm glad your mom is okay and is on the mend. I'm going
to get some sleep. I'll talk to you tomorrow?"

"Yeah, fine. Talk to you later. Bye." He hangs up before I
even get the chance to respond. I roll my eyes, turn off the light,
and let sleep pull me under.

CHAPTER 16

TRISTAN

*I*t's been a week since Lana returned from England, and while we have talked, things have been tense between us. I don't know if it's the distance or the time apart that's killing me. I know she can feel something's wrong, too. She's been different since we talked last week.

Construction will start on the new cabins in a few weeks, and I've asked Lana to come back out to oversee everything. She arrives at the beginning of the month and will be here for an undetermined amount of time. Her boss is allowing her to work remotely in the meantime, and I want everything to be perfect. I need this time with her. I need to show her that things can work between us. I still haven't figured out how, but it has to.

I need her.

Mom is home from the hospital, and all of us, including Holden, have been waiting on her hand and foot. I need her to get better, and the medicine the doctors have put her on is making her weak. She hardly gets out of bed, and when she does, it's because she needs to move around and

Dad or I help her. She sleeps a lot, and I'm worried about her.

There's a court date set up for the asshole that hit her, unless he pleads and takes a deal. Thank God he had insurance on his car, at least, and they are covering her medical expenses. It's some guy from out of town, Aaron O'Keefe. He was here on a work trip and had one too many. It was still pretty early in the evening, so he drank a lot in a short while.

I dial Lana's number, needing to hear her voice, and it goes to voicemail after only one ring. She ignored my call. Her beautiful voice floats through the phone, asking me to leave a message and she will call me back.

"Lana. I need to hear your voice, babe. Mom is doing okay, but I'm worried about her. Please, call me back." I go to hang up and put the phone back to my ear. "Also, I miss that sexy ass of yours, and I can't wait until you get here so I can fill you up. I miss you so damn much, Lana. Call me."

I wonder how long I'll have to wait for her to call me back this time?

Lana arrives today, and I am crawling out of my skin with excitement. The contracts have been drawn up with the construction company, and ground-breaking is tomorrow. I was even able to secure a small article in the local paper about the expansion, so people know what's going on. Her flight should be here in another hour, and I don't want to be late.

I pull on a nice pair of jeans and a button-down top. I match it with my cowboy hat and smile at my reflection. She's always loved the cowboy hat. I plan on swinging by the florist to pick up some flowers for her, and then we can go to my apartment and get reunited. Everything is working out to plan.

Except, when she arrives, she's not alone. And she didn't tell me she wasn't coming alone. There's a man walking with her, and the two of them are laughing as they enter the baggage area. She sees me, and her eyes light up. I sheepishly look down at the flowers in my hand and back at her.

"Tristan." She walks up to me and takes the flowers. "Are these for me?"

I nod and speak quietly. "I didn't know you weren't coming alone. I wouldn't have brought flowers if I had known."

She scrunches her face. "What are you talking about?" She looks at the man she was walking with and motions toward him. "Charlie? I met him on the plane. We didn't come here together."

Boy, do I feel like an idiot. I look at the ground and shake my head. "Sorry." Ever since I found out she went to England for her job, and Russ was behind it, I've been paranoid. I feel like he's trying to drive a wedge between us all over again. If I'm being honest with myself, I'm scared of losing her.

"It's fine. Let me get my bag, and we can get on our way."

The ride to my apartment is silent, and the air between us is thick with tension. I can't stand it anymore. "What's wrong? Things have been different between us since your trip to England."

She shrugs. "Nothing's wrong with me. You're the one who's been different."

Have I? I think back to the conversations we've had over the past month. I've given her updates about Mom and the ranch. We've talked about Holden. We've had phone sex a few times. Nothing out of the ordinary. Except, almost every conversation we've had has been about me. I'll ask her questions here and there about work, but whenever she tries to tell me about the Carringtons' remodel, I shut her down.

"Shit." She nods her head when I don't add anything else.

She knows I've figured it out. "Why not tell me sooner?"

She shrugs again but keeps looking straight ahead. "I tried. You shut me down, and then it was easier to not talk about it. This project and that one are consuming all my time. Simone's remodel will be complete in another few weeks. I'm going to have to leave here to go there for the final bit and make sure she's happy. I told her I would."

"What?" I panic, knowing she's going to leave sooner than I thought. I rub my chest and slow my racing heart, then I take a few deep breaths and gather my thoughts. "I was expecting you to stay a while. I didn't know you had to leave early."

"You would have if you ever let me talk about it," she mumbles.

I know she's right, but it doesn't sting any less. I toss my hat in the back seat of my truck and rub my hand over my hair. I'm fucking this whole thing up. I have too much going on. I'm trying to balance everything, but I'm not doing well.

I pull into the parking lot at my complex and throw the truck in park. I turn to face her.

"Lana, I'm sorry. Russ is a sensitive subject with me, and with everything going on with my mom and the ranch, it's been hard. It's difficult for me to be away from you. Every time we take two steps forward, I feel we take three back. I take a lot of that responsibility, and I'm sorry. I miss you like crazy. I want to wrap you in my arms every night and wake up to your smiling face every day.

"Being apart is a lot harder for me than I thought it would be. I got two days with you before I was forced back here, away from *you*. Then, you went to England to see Russ—"

"I didn't go to *see him*," she says through clenched teeth. "I had a job to do. That's what happens when someone has a job. I did what my boss asked me to do. It's not like I had a choice."

She's not getting it. My frustration is through the roof. I run my hands through my hair, tugging the ends, the sting a welcome feeling. My blood boils, and my heartbeat drums in my ears so loud I can barely hear myself. She has no idea how much I want to rip that man's head off. Even the mention of his name makes me go crazy. "Oh, so, if your boss asked you to jump off a bridge, would you?" I yell back.

"Fuck you, Tristan." She scoffs and pushes open the door.

"Where are you going?" I ask, climbing out just as fast.

"Calling an Uber to take me to a hotel. I'm not staying here. I've been in town for an hour, and we are already screaming at one another! How are we going to survive my trip here?"

"No. Shit." I clench my hands and lock my jaw as I rack my brain on how to fix this. "Please don't. I'm sorry."

"You say that a lot. Are you sure you understand the meaning of the word?"

I reach out for her and take her hand in mine. When she doesn't pull out of my grasp, I know I have a chance to fix things. "There's a lot going on, and I'm stressed out. Can we please go inside to talk? I promise to listen to everything you tell me."

She takes a step closer to me, wraps her hand around the back of my neck, and pulls me down to her, our lips connecting in a fierce kiss. There is so much want and need behind the kiss. When we finally break, she sways a little. I drop my forehead to hers, and the two of us breathe one another in.

"Hey, cowboy," she coos.

"Hey, beautiful. Does this mean you'll stay?" She nods her head and bites her lip, smiling. "Thank God." I grab her hand and drag her toward my apartment.

"Wait, what about my bag?" She reaches behind her like she's trying to mentally drag it with her.

"Later. I want to be inside you. Then, once you're thoroughly fucked, I'll come back to get it."

I push open the front door and drag her down the hall to my bedroom. My apartment doesn't have much in the way of homey touches, but it's enough. I have a few pictures on my walls of my family and friends and the ranch. No flowers, no colored things. It's very bland—white walls, white kitchen cabinets, and brown carpet.

The only room I've done anything with is my bedroom. I blew up some pictures Kasey took of the horses and mounted those on my wall. I have some hand-me-down furniture I found at one of the thrift stores that just needed new stain, and a king-sized bed with a navy comforter. I wanted a big comfortable bed. I work long hours at the ranch, and I come home and crash most nights.

I pull her body flush with mine, my hands exploring every warm curve of her body, while my lips draw delectable moans and whimpers from her mouth. God, it's been too long since I've had her under me, since I've been in control of her pleasure. Last time, it was too short, and I'm going to make up for it now.

I pull her blouse over her head and help her push her skinny jeans down off her hips and down her legs. She kicks off her flats and finishes pulling them off around her ankles. She stands before me in a sexy little black lace bra and matching thong.

"You look good enough to eat," I mumble against her lips, unable to keep my fingers and mouth off of her.

"Feast away, cowboy," she says, pushing my head down her body. Every time she calls me cowboy, it stirs something else in me. More than a primal need for her. I finish sinking to my knees and pull her panties to the side, diving into her, lapping up everything she offers me. She holds my head for balance as I toss her leg over my shoulder for a better angle.

When I insert two fingers, I know she's close. I feel it with how her body responds to mine and the moans of pleasure coming from her. I want her on top of me. I pull my face away, and when she tries to put me back where she needs me the most, I nip her thigh.

"I want you to ride me. Be the cowgirl I know you want to be." I smirk when her cheeks redden.

I pull my clothes off in record time and lie on the bed. I hold my hand out to her, watching as she unclasps her bra and slides her panties down her legs, giving me a show to remember. She gives a little shake of her hips as she bends at her waist to pull them off. She then dangles them from her index finger, showing them to me.

Fuck. She's so hot.

She climbs on the bed, lines herself up with me, and sinks down slowly. My hands automatically go to her hips as she controls the pace and depth in which she takes me. Her hands rest on my chest for extra support, and she's lost in the moment. Being able to watch her pleasure herself using me is on an entirely different playing field.

She's so lost in the sensations that, when I reach my thumb out to brush it along her hard clit, she moans and comes almost instantly on me. I help control her movements, extending her orgasm, and when she's come down enough, I thrust up into her, hard, chasing my own release. As I watch her boobs bounce, she tightens around me again.

"Come on, baby. Come like a good girl," I request.

She bites her lip and reaches between us to play with herself. The moment she starts coming, I let go, filling her. We both moan and wriggle through our orgasms before she collapses on me. I rub her back, feeling our racing hearts beating together. I kiss the side of her head, and she turns to look at me, a smile on her face.

"I love you, Lana. Not a doubt in my mind."

CHAPTER 17

LANA

*C*onstruction day. My favorite day of every project. I love the thrill of getting to see my designs finally come to fruition. I've been working with a few designers in Boston for the furniture, and I've been informed by the construction company it should take about six months to finish. Perfect timing for the winter guests to come out for snow and skiing.

Today, the crews will be digging to lay the initial foundation. Mr. and Mrs. Ellis had the area cleared years ago for the new cabins, but they had never started construction. It was easy to get the crew out here over the past month to level it all out so they can start construction today, instead of having to do all the leg work.

Tristan woke early and has been pacing his apartment, nervous to start everything. I gave him an orgasm this morning to help calm his nerves, and he gave me two just for being so nice. I could definitely get used to this. I pull my jeans up, and they feel a little snug around the waist. Must be all the good food Tristan is forcing down my throat. I ate so much yesterday

I could barely walk. If I continue to eat like this, I'm going to leave here fifty pounds heavier.

I gather everything I need, load up Tristan's truck, and climb in. It's still early, and the crew won't be arriving for another hour or so. That gives me plenty of time to look over the plans and iron out any issues that may arise.

My stomach rumbles, and I rub it, willing it to be quiet as Tristan hops in. He notices me rubbing my belly, and he smiles.

"Hungry, or not feeling well?"

"A little of both. You're feeding me too much. I'm getting used to having all this food now, and my body is revolting against me." I laugh.

"I'm sure we can find you something at the ranch. Mom makes some mean cinnamon rolls."

His smile fades at the mention of his mom. She wasn't in the hospital that long, but she's changed a lot since she's been back. I know he's worried about her, and I wish there was something I could do to help. I'm actually hoping he'll let me see her at some point today so I can say hi and spend some time with her. She has always been so kind to me; I know this is a huge burden on his family.

"She's going to be okay, Tristan." I take his hand in mine and give him a reassuring squeeze, then kiss the back of his knuckles.

"I know. I just need my mom back. I want her to be around long enough to hopefully see me get married and meet her grandchildren." He glances at me and smirks. *Is he picturing marrying me?*

Lana Ellis. It does have a nice ring to it. I spend the entire ride to the ranch daydreaming about my perfect wedding. I don't even realize we've pulled up until he cuts the engine. We both get out, and I look around the land with a new perspective. I could see myself raising kids here with this man. The only problem is my job and family are back east.

Mom would kill me if I moved here and never made it home to visit with grandkids. And what about my job? I've been lucky, but I won't be able to work remotely forever. Eloise would never allow that.

"Hey, where'd you go? You seem lost in thoughts."

"Nothing," I lie. "Just trying to picture the land with the new cabins and what it will do to this place." I smile up at him. "I'm so happy you are doing this and that I'm a part of it. Thanks for hiring my company."

"I'm so glad it was you, Lana." He wraps his arms around me and buries his head in the crook of my neck, placing gentle kisses along my skin.

"All right, you two. Get a room," Holden chortles behind us.

"You're just jealous, man," Tristan says, ignoring his friend as he continues to kiss me.

I finally manage to push him away and give Holden a hug. "Good to see you so happy," he murmurs against my shoulder before releasing me.

"You too. Now, point me in the direction of food. I'm starving and need something to eat."

He looks at Tristan. "Didn't you feed this girl when she got here?"

"Sure did, we've been working up quite an appetite." He smirks, and I smack him in the arm in embarrassment.

"I'm sure Holden doesn't want to know what we are doing," I mumble as I rub my reddened cheeks.

I leave the two of them talking and go in search of food. Tristan sends me inside the house to find something in the kitchen, and when I walk in, his mom is sitting at the table. "Hi, Mrs. Ellis." I smile at her.

Her face brightens, and she extends her right arm for me to give her a hug. She has a cast on her leg, and her left arm is in a sling. "Lana, welcome back, dear." I wrap my arms around her gently and pull back. "We're so happy to have you here. Tristan hasn't talked about anything but you coming back for days."

We spend the next few minutes talking as I gather some food, and it feels so normal. She's so easy to talk to. When I finish my banana and peanut butter crackers, I put my plate in the dishwasher and tell her I'll be back to visit later. She waves me out, and I watch her smile turn down before I leave the front door.

"Tristan?" I call for him as I step on the front porch.

I see Holden, and he motions toward where the new build will be. I walk down the path and stop a few feet away when I see him talking to the foreman, Steve. His hands rest easily on his hips, and his muscles ripple under his snug t-shirt. *Damn, I want to tear that thing off him.*

"Lana, right?" a man asks from behind me. I turn to see Emmett standing there with a yellow hard hat on, light-colored jeans, and a loose t-shirt.

I smile. "Hey. Emmett, right?" He nods. "It's nice to see you again."

"So, this was your project?" He gestures to the empty area in front of us. "I remember you told me you were doing the designs last time."

"Yeah, Tristan hired my firm."

He nods and looks around. "Hey, listen, if you're not still seeing Holden, I'd love to go out for drinks or dinner sometime if you're interested?"

I play with the bottom of my shirt. It's not like I'm actually thinking of going on a date with the guy, but I'm trying to find a way to let him down gently without making it seem like there is a conflict of interest. Technically, sleeping with the client doesn't break any rules, but it doesn't look great either.

"Actually, I'm not available. I'm only here for a little while, and then I am heading overseas to finish work with another client. I'm going to be swamped while I'm here."

His smile fades, but he has the good grace to try and not look too hurt. "All right, see ya around then," he says and walks away to join some of the other workers.

"Lana, come meet Don Martineau, the manager," Tristan calls over for me.

He places his hand on my lower back as I stand next to him, and I brush it off. While on site, we need to maintain a level of professionalism. Don is a nice man and seems to have a lot of experience under his belt. He tells me the plans for the day and how far he hopes to get. As long as the weather stays nice, there shouldn't be a problem with staying on schedule.

The rest of the crew arrives, along with all the heavy machinery, and they get to work digging the hole for the foundation. There's not a lot for me to do at this point, so after watching the men work for an hour or so, I take a walk around the property.

Tristan and Holden are helping some of the guests, and Mr. Ellis is taking care of his wife. I should sit down to do some work, but my mind isn't in it. Instead, I pull out a sketchbook and decorate a mock-up of Tristan's apartment. It was so bare when I walked in last night; it almost made me sad. I'd love to be able to help him add a feminine touch to it.

He finds me sitting by the water as I put the finishing touches on the living room, and he takes a seat next to me. He kisses my cheek and pulls the sketchpad from my lap to look at what I'm drawing.

"What's this?"

"I wanted to redesign your apartment. Make it look more

like a home. It feels so cold and unwelcoming there." I pretend to shiver and smile at him.

He stares at the drawing, tracing his finger over my design. "I love it," he murmurs.

I beam. "Really? You mean it?"

He pulls me to him for a hard kiss. "Yes, really. I'd like it if you add a bit of you to the apartment. When can you start?"

"We can go to the store and see if we can find some of the stuff I need, and then I will also look online and connect with some people I know."

Construction has been going on for almost two weeks now, and I've been working up a storm trying to get the rest of his apartment set up. A few pieces of artwork arrived today, so I took his truck back to the apartment to meet the delivery guy. He was kind enough to wait until I unboxed everything and took the trash out with him. He also got a huge tip for doing so, so he definitely wasn't complaining.

Tristan has been dealing with a lot, and I wanted to do something nice for him and cook dinner. These past few weeks have felt very domestic, and I'd be lying if I didn't say I've enjoyed it. I walk up and down the grocery store aisles, picking up anything I might need to cook.

When I reach the tampons, I freeze. *When was the last time I had my period?* I try to mentally do the calculations in my head as my heart races and my stomach flips. Has it really been six weeks? It must be off because of all the traveling, right?

I reach a shaking hand up to the pregnancy tests and put a box in my cart. The happy, smiling woman on the box taunts me as I finish my shopping. Do I take it now? Do I wait until morning? I don't think I'm going to be able to wait that long.

Okay, Lana. Calm down. There's nothing to worry about until I take the test.

He won't be home for another few hours, so I can take it without him knowing and will figure out what I'm going to do only if it comes out positive. I finish shopping, load up the truck, and get home as fast as I can. I put everything away and open the pink box.

Easy. Pee on a stick. I can do this.

I watch the initial line appear and close my eyes, too afraid to look. I'll wait for the three-minute timer to go off. Until then, I'm not even sure it's accurate. I jump when my phone's timer rings and hurry to turn the annoying sound off. I hold my breath as I open my eyes and look.

Two. Pink. Lines.

My breath comes into my lungs in short, labored pants. I'm not even sure I'm getting oxygen in because I'm freaking out so bad. Oh my God! What the hell am I going to do? We can't have a baby. This wasn't supposed to happen. I dial Beth's number.

"Hey, what's going on?" she answers.

"Beth." I pause to take a breath. "I'm pregnant."

"Are you fucking kidding me?" she screams into the phone. I have to pull it away from my ear so she doesn't make me go deaf. "Lana, you're kidding, right?"

"Beth, what am I going to do?" The tears are streaming down my cheeks, and I sniffle, trying to rein everything in.

"Is it Tristan's?" I scoff. Did she seriously ask me that? "I just wanted to double-check," she says when I don't respond right away.

"Yes. I haven't slept with anyone else. I take my birth control, though. How is this possible?"

"It happens. I've heard other stories of it, too. It's going to be fine. Does he know yet?"

I shake my head but then remember she can't see me. "No. I just took it. He's still at the ranch."

God, this explains so much now—the bloat, how tired I've been, how hungry I've been. It all lines up. How am I going to explain this to him? He's not ready to have a family. Or is it me who's not ready? I'm twenty-eight years old. I wanted to get my life and career nailed down before I settled down and started a family. My plan was to get married at thirty and have kids by thirty-two. Not now!

I finish my phone call with Beth and promise to tell her what happens when I tell Tristan. I wipe the tears from my eyes and start researching everything about pregnancy. I have no idea what I'm doing or how to start this. I do know I'll need to make an appointment with my doctor to get checked out.

Do I find a doctor out here? My home is in Massachusetts, but Tristan is here. There's no way he can leave his home and the ranch, but I don't think I'm ready to uproot my life to move here. I like being an east coast girl. I like my friends, my job, my life. On the other hand, I love Tristan and his family, and I love this ranch. I've pictured a cute little boy who looks like Tristan on many occasions, running around the ranch, laughing.

Tristan would be a good father, I know it. I'm just not ready to tell him yet. After England. That will be easier. I can do this. I hide the box of tests under the sink and bury the positive test in the trash.

CHAPTER 18

TRISTAN

*C*onstruction is going great. My apartment also looks amazing—thanks to Lana's personal touches— and Mom is doing much better. Everything is looking up, except for the fact that Lana is leaving for England and then Massachusetts today. I don't want her to go. I've gotten used to having her here, so it's difficult to let her leave.

Having her here for two weeks isn't enough. I wish I could ask her to move here forever, but we are still trying to figure us out. *Would she want to?* Could this ranch and the life I could give her be enough? She's successful in Boston, and I don't want to ask her to give it all up for me, even though my heart is begging me to.

She rolls her suitcase behind her and into the living room. She looks around at the walls that are now brimming with life, and she smiles.

"Not to toot my own horn, but *damn!*" she says and adds a quiet chuckle for good measure.

I pull her into my arms and hold her tight. "Yeah, it looks amazing in here. Thank you."

She wiggles out of my grasp and nods. "You're welcome. Now, I've got a plane to catch, and I need you to get me to the airport with plenty of time for my flight."

"I know," I respond sadly. "I'm not ready to say goodbye. It's going to be another five months before I see you again. What do you expect me to do with myself?"

She smiles and places her hand on my cheek. I revel in the feel of her touch. "Things have a way of working out." She kisses me hard on the lips and pulls back. "Come on. I've got to go."

We ride in silence, each of us consumed with our own thoughts. She keeps playing with the hem of her shirt and tucking hair behind her ear. Something is definitely eating at her, and I need to make sure she isn't having second thoughts about trying to make a long-distance relationship work. We've talked about it on and off over the past two weeks, and she seems guarded whenever we discuss it. She says she's open to it, but there seems to be something she's not telling me.

"Lana, is everything okay? You're making me a bit nervous over here," I ask, trying to keep my tone casual.

She stops wringing her fingers and plasters a smile on her face. "Of course. Why wouldn't it be?"

"You play with your shirt and your hair when you have something on your mind. You've done both this whole ride."

She waves her hands in front of her as we reach the curb. "Oh, I'm just worried about this project. I'm only gone for two days to see the final touches put into place and confirm she's happy with what we're doing for her. That's not a lot of time to make changes if she's not happy."

I narrow my eyes in her direction as I help her with her bag. "You sure that's it?"

She nods and hums her response before wrapping her arms

around me in a big hug and kissing me. "Tristan, you love me, right?" she asks, uncertainty lacing her words.

Where is all this coming from? "You know I do, Lana."

"Good. I love you, too, Tristan. I'll text you when I land. It will be early morning for you."

She waves goodbye and is through the sliding glass doors before I can get another word out. *Strangest damn conversation I've ever had.* Holden calls me, asking to stop by the ranch for the night to help with the guests since it's movie night, and I'm happy not to spend it alone in my apartment. At least, this way, I will be able to get my mind off Lana.

The movie finishes by ten o'clock, and some of our guests are basically walking zombies at this point. The damn city slickers aren't used to all this fresh air and outdoor activities. Throws people for a loop; they aren't expecting to want to nap for half the day.

We get everyone back safely, and I say good night to Mom and Dad then head home. I know she won't be in England yet, but I miss her like crazy. *How the hell can I miss someone so damn much?* I pull up her Instagram account and scroll through the pictures she's posted.

There aren't many with me, but there is one when I stayed with her in Boston that I adore. It's the two of us by the Charles River. She said she wanted a selfie of us, and right before she took it, I kissed her hard on the cheek. She was laughing so hard, and I started blowing raspberries against her skin, just to keep hearing her laughter.

I see pictures of her from college with friends, and even some with other guys. I scroll past those as fast as I can. I don't need the reminder that she's been with other people. If I didn't fuck things up all those years ago, she could have been with me. Hell, we could be married with a family right now if that's what she would have wanted.

I would give that girl the world if it means I get to keep her. If it means she gets to come home to me every night and goes to sleep next to me. At this point, I'd even be willing to give up the ranch so we don't have to spend it apart.

Running my fingers through my hair, I tug the ends in frustration. *This is so fucked up.* I've never wanted anything but to run the damn ranch. To make people see how amazing it is—make them see it how I see it. I want her more than that, though. I know now there is no way my life will be complete without her in it. I feel like myself when she's with me.

I call Holden, and before he can even say hello, I state, "I can't be without her for the next few months. What if she comes out here to finalize the plans, and that's it? What if I can't convince her to stay? What if she doesn't love me as much as I love her? Holden, I went ten years without her, thinking I was happy, but I haven't been. I've only been going through the motions."

"Dude, what the hell are you going on about? You know it's almost midnight, right? I have company. I'll talk to you tomorrow when you're not drunk."

"I'm not—"

The line goes dead before I can finish, and when I pull it away from my ear, the call ended screen flashes before turning dark again. I need to make some grand gesture to show her I'm serious about trying to make us work. I pull a notebook out and jot two ideas down before I yawn and want to close my eyes.

1. **Move to Massachusetts.**
2. **Propose to Lana.**

Neither is doable yet, considering we've only been dating for a little over a month, and most of that has been long-distance. I toss my notebook to the other side of the couch and head to the bathroom to shower so I can get to bed.

The bar of soap is almost gone, so I dig under the sink, looking for another bar. I grab a box and notice bright pink. *Must be some tampons or something.* I smirk, thinking she's just embarrassed about having them around. She doesn't have to hide them; it's not that big of a deal.

I pull the box out and stare at it for a solid minute before my mind registers what it is—an opened box of pregnancy tests. The front says there are two tests in the box, and when I look inside, one is missing. I sit on the toilet seat and stare at the box in confusion.

Was she ever going to tell me? If she had a scare, I'd want to know so we could be more careful. It had to be negative, right? She didn't want to scare me, so she took the test and tossed it because it was nothing to worry about. I look at the small trash can next to me, contemplating my next move.

She wouldn't have tossed it in here, would she?

I lean over and dig through the tissues on top until I see an opaque pink plastic top. My hand shakes as I reach for it and pull it out of the trash.

Two lines.

I start to breathe heavily and push a shaking hand through my hair. I close my eyes, trying to calm my racing heart. Two lines means negative, right? *No, that's not right.* One line is no; two lines is yes.

Lana is fucking pregnant and hasn't said a fucking word to me. She left here, flew to another country, carrying my child. My earlier tiredness is gone and has been replaced by full-on anger and adrenaline. I carry the life-changing stick into the bedroom and pace, trying to come up with a good excuse for her not to tell me. After pacing for a solid ten minutes, there's not a single explanation in the world that makes enough sense.

Is she not going to keep it? Is that why she didn't want to tell me? Is she afraid I'll get mad? *Is it even mine?* Fuck. This whole thing is so fucked up. I always imagined I'd be married for at least a year, have a nice house, and then be able to surprise Mom and Dad with the news that they are finally going to be grandparents.

It's almost two in the morning. I need to get a little bit of sleep if I'm going to be at the ranch in the morning. I take the fastest shower known to man and climb into bed in just my boxers. I place my hand under my head and take a deep breath.

"What the hell are you thinking, Lana?" I ask to the empty room. I close my eyes and wait for sleep to take me under.

Until I speak with Lana, I don't want to tell anyone about this, especially Holden. I love him like a brother, but he's got a big mouth at times, and I don't want this to get back to my mom and dad. This day seems to be going on forever, though. Lana texted me when she landed, and I fought the urge to yell at her when I got it.

She told me she would call later, but she won't be able to stay on the phone for long. Her flight back to Massachusetts is tomorrow afternoon, and she told me she wanted to make sure Mrs. Carrington was happy before she left. I've been watching the time tick so slowly that at times I've thought it was moving backward.

Finally, after dealing with the construction crew and the guests, the moment of truth has arrived. Will she come clean and confess, or will it be just another secret? I swipe the call to answer it.

"Hi, Lana."

CHAPTER 19

LANA

"Tristan," I breathe. "I'm so happy to hear your voice. I miss you so much." Relief washes over me. I've been anxious all day, and hearing his voice settles me. When he doesn't respond, I continue. "She loved it. She absolutely loved all my designs." I can't keep the smile from my face.

"That's great. I'm happy for you."

"Yes. She has a friend that works for a fashion magazine who wants to do a showcase piece on my remodel for her next issue. *Smith and Quill Designs* is going to be huge. They will probably have to open more offices in order to keep up!"

I pace around my room, unable to contain my excitement. I've tried sitting and being calm, but I'm not able to. I want to dance and shout from the rooftops. *I'm in England. Maybe I can pretend to be a chimney sweep like in Mary Poppins.*

"Wow, that's awesome," he says. Except it doesn't sound like it's awesome. It sounds like something is seriously wrong.

My mood changes instantly. "Tristan, what's wrong?"

He takes a deep breath and pushes it out. "Nothing. I've had a long day, and I barely slept last night. I had a lot on my mind." He attempts to lighten his tone. "I'm happy for you." The silence stretches between us before he says, "Anything else you want to tell me?"

Do I? I mean, besides getting a positive pregnancy test, but I have no idea what I'm doing about that. I rub my still flat belly and look down at it. I still need to confirm the test was accurate. Maybe the tests were bad. "No," I say, dragging the word out. "Not that I can think of."

"Okay," he answers matter-of-factly. "I've got to go. Have a safe flight tomorrow."

That's it? No, *I'll talk to you tomorrow?* No, *we will work on a long-distance relationship shit?* He hangs up before I can respond, and I stare at my phone in disbelief until the screen goes dark. My mind runs in circles as I run through the conversation. *He must be tired,* the voice of reason pipes up. We've told one another we love each other, and I am trying to find a way for us to make things work. He knows that.

What is he doing to make things work? That quiet voice of insecurity sneaks in, and now I'm contemplating what exactly he would be giving up. I'm the one who would have to move for him. I'm the one who would have to find a new job. I'm the one to leave friends and family if we are going to make this work.

It's me. I have to give up everything for him.

Maybe I don't want to give up my entire life for him and this baby. I like my life just the way it is. I don't need this baby messing anything up. Tristan and I are already struggling to make things work; adding a baby into the mix seems like a disaster.

I place my hands over my stomach and rub. It's crazy to think there is a little baby growing inside me. I'd never know except for my boobs hurt like a bitch, and I alternate between starving and being sick. I haven't told my parents yet because I want bloodwork to prove it. Although, after some online research, there is no way to get a false positive. It just doesn't happen.

As soon as I get back home, I'm getting the bloodwork to prove it.

I've been staring at a wall since the nurse from my doctor's office called to congratulate me on my upcoming baby. I have to call my OB and make an appointment, but I can't drag myself to do it. I would never abort, and this baby will be loved and cherished, even if his or her dad isn't in the picture. I can't imagine Tristan not being part of their lives, but since it's been a week since he's talked with me, I have to assume he doesn't want me.

Since he won't answer any of my calls, Eloise had to call and try to speak with him. He wouldn't answer her call either, so I had to call Steve for an update. Seems they have run into a little bout of trouble with some pipes where the foundation is supposed to go, but it shouldn't take them too long to correct it.

I just want to drink. I do the next best thing and pull a tub of *Ben and Jerry's Phish Food* from my freezer. I dig in while watching a cheesy romantic comedy. Except what should be funny is actually sad and depressing. I spend the rest of my evening crying as I stuff my face. I look down at my phone when it lights up, and Holden's name comes up.

"What?" I answer, my mouth full of ice cream.

"What happened between you and Tristan?"

He's going to try to blame this on me? I go on the defense, my shoulders rising to my ears as I put the ice cream down on the counter with a little too much force. The spoon jumps out of the container and lands on the carpet. "What did *I* do?" I scoff. "Ask your buddy. I didn't do a damned thing. He's the one who won't answer my calls or texts."

"When I asked, he said to ask you because you're the one with all the secrets."

I throw my hands up. "What the fuck is he talking about? He's the one who's being secretive. I've tried to talk to him. I've tried to figure out what I *possibly* did now that he won't talk to me."

I hear rustling on the other end of the phone, and Tristan's voice comes on. "You didn't tell me you were pregnant. That's what you did wrong," he yells into the phone.

Everything comes to a stop. I take a deep breath in, but I have to fight to release it. My hands shake, and the television goes silent. All I can hear is his steady breathing on the other end of the line.

"How'd you know?" I whisper.

"Whose is it?" he asks, venom dripping from his words. His speech is slurred.

Did he seriously just ask me that? The tears fall down my cheeks as I take in a breath to be able to answer him. I open my mouth and close it twice before I'm able to squeak a response past my dry throat. "You seriously think it's anyone but yours?" I guess I really am doing this alone. I straighten my spine and wipe my tears. I'm pissed. "Go to hell, Tristan. I don't want you to have any part of this baby's life. For all he or she will know, you were an anonymous sperm donor. Don't call, don't check in on me. We'll be just fine without you."

I hang up the phone. The hurt at his words cuts deep. I feel raw, lifeless after our brief conversation. The noise from the TV slowly comes back, and the red haze around my vision dissipates as my body relaxes again.

"Looks like it's just you and me, kid," I say. My phone rings, and I don't have to look at it to know it's Tristan. I answer. "Call me again, and I'll put a restraining order against you."

"You can't keep my kid away from me." He seems to have sobered up real fast.

"It's a good thing you live so far away. Lose my number, asshole."

I toss the nearly empty container of ice cream in the trash and clean up the mess on my carpet before I take a shower and climb into bed. I leave my phone in the living room. I'm afraid if I take it to the bedroom with me, I'll answer his calls. I know Tristan enough to know he won't stop, especially now the cat is out of the bag.

We've had enough conversations, so I know he wants kids and a family. He wants the whole package, but he hasn't learned to pull his head out of his ass. I can't believe he is pulling this shit on me. Didn't he learn from his past mistakes to trust me? Why is it that I'm the one he always doubts?

Tristan tries to get a hold of me at the office no less than three times. I make Hannah send him to my voicemail each time. I'll call him back when I've had time to cool my head. I made sure his call wasn't urgent by contacting Steve and talking with him for a few minutes. Eloise seems to be butting her head into this project more than usual, and it's really starting to irritate me.

Of course, that could also be the raging amount of hormones coursing through my body. My boobs hurt, my back hurts, and I just want to sleep. This baby is sucking everything out of me. And the worst part is my parents haven't seen me in a while, so I agreed to show up for dinner this weekend. I need someone else in my court, and I know my parents will support me through anything.

I walk through their front door and call out a greeting. Mom shouts back that she's in the kitchen. I climb the stairs to my old bedroom and drop my overnight bag off. It takes me a few hours to get to my childhood home from Boston, and it's easier to stay the night when I come.

I walk into the kitchen and see Mom cooking up a storm. We give each other a hug, and she kisses my cheek, instantly making me feel better.

"What's wrong, pumpkin? You seem stressed."

Yeah, you could say that. "Where's Dad? I have something I want to tell both of you."

She puts the spatula down and slowly turns to me. "Is this good news or bad news?"

I shrug. "I guess that depends on who you are."

Dad's ears must have been ringing because he walks into the room a minute later. Although, he always has had pretty perfect timing. They sit at the table with me, and I tell them my story from the beginning. And when I say beginning, I mean, I go way back. I tell them about our vacation, and how I fell in love with Tristan—even back then. I skirt over the part about him taking my virginity because that's not something they need to know.

So, when I bring up what's been going on recently, and how I got hired for the remodel, there's no shock when I explain how we have been trying to make things work again. The shock comes when I tell them I'm almost two months pregnant with his child.

"Does he know?" Mom asks.

I nod. "Yeah, he knows," I answer solemnly. I push a disbelieving snort through my nose. "He actually asked me whose it is because I didn't tell him. I hid the test. I was going to tell him once I confirmed everything with the doctor. I wanted to really be sure before I turned his life upside down, too."

They ask me a few more questions, and we talk a little longer. I feel better, and even feel a little bad for blowing up at

Tristan like I did. I can only imagine what he felt like when he saw the test with no explanation. *But he also asked if it was someone else's like I've been sleeping around.* He knows me better than that—or I thought he did.

I haven't heard from him since the blowout, and it's not like his number is blocked. He just hasn't reached out. Although, to be fair, I told him if he did, I'd put a restraining order against him, and I also told him to lose my number. I bite the bullet and open a text to him. I'm not ready to hear his husky voice, but I do need to talk to him.

Me: *Hey.*

Tristan: *Hey. I'm glad you're contacting me. Can we talk?*

I type a response, then delete it and try again. When the words don't come out the way I expect them to, I give up and put my phone down for the night without responding to him.

CHAPTER 20

TRISTAN

I'm going out of my mind. She messaged, and when I asked to talk, she didn't respond. We need to figure stuff out. Are we going to have joint custody? Will she move out here? I refuse to not be part of my son or daughter's life. Family is way too important to me to not have this—even if she doesn't want me. She has a part of me growing inside her, though, and there's nothing that will ever change that bond we share.

I look at the clock. It's past midnight there, and she's probably sleeping by now. I resign myself to having to wait until the next morning to call her. I lie in bed and can't get her out of my damn mind. Has she gone to any doctor's appointments? I always pictured myself going to the ultrasounds, holding my wife's hand, and letting this be something we experience together.

I would never have thought it would be Lana. How fucked up is fate? It pushes us back together after all these years, just to pull us apart again. I've already made the grand gesture once and went to see her to amend things. I don't want to be flying out to Boston every time I fuck up to fix things.

Knowing myself, I might as well live out there. I'm always putting my foot in my mouth. Point in case. If I wasn't drunk and hurt, I never would have asked her if the kid was mine. I knew from the moment I saw that test that no one else had touched her. I know she wouldn't do that to me, especially when I know her views on relationships and cheating.

If she won't come to me, I'm going to have to go to her. I might as well get an airline credit card. I'm going to be a part of this baby's life, even if I have to fly out every weekend to do it.

My phone rings early the next morning, and I groan as I reach for it. Lana's name flashes on the screen, and I sit straight up, sleep now forgotten.

"Lana?"

"Hey, Tristan."

I run my fingers through my hair as I try to shake the sleep from my voice. "I'm glad you called. I'm sorry I asked you that. I know the baby is mine; I just don't know why you hid it from me." She sighs. "Where are you right now?"

"Lying in bed, staring at the ceiling. Why?"

I lie down on my back and stare at my darkened ceiling. "If I close my eyes and concentrate, it's almost like you're here." I put my hand under my head and continue. "Why didn't you tell me?"

"I wanted to make sure. I thought maybe the results were wrong or something. I didn't want to scare you or force you into anything if it wasn't even true. Then you wouldn't take any of my calls, and I had no idea you knew about the test until you called me while drunk."

I scrunch my face. "Not one of my finest moments. I'm sorry for that. I didn't understand how you could hide something so monumental from me."

"Yeah, well, imagine how I felt."

"Tell me how you felt, Lana." The quiet request falls from my lips. I wait patiently as she gathers her thoughts.

"Like my life was ending and beginning all at the same time. I've pictured a mini version of you running around so many times, but I didn't think it would happen." She laughs dryly. "I was afraid things would end like last time because we live so far away. Except now," she hesitates, "well, now I guess they can't, huh?"

"No. They can't. Fate brought you back into my life, and I'll be damned if I sit by and do nothing to try to keep you in it. Have you had any doctor's appointments yet? Any ultrasounds?"

She takes in a shaky breath. "No."

"Please, don't cry, Lana." My heart breaks, knowing I'm not there to console her. To take away a fraction of the pain she feels.

"I don't want to do this alone, Tristan," she whispers.

The emotions she's feeling hit me hard. I don't want her to do it alone, either. I don't want her to give up her life, family, and friends, but I can't give up the ranch. It's been in my family for generations, and my parents would kill me if I sold it to live in Boston.

"I know, babe. We'll figure it out. I'm going to come out for a little bit. I want to be there for you and the baby."

She sniffles. "Really? You'll come out here?"

How could I say no to her? "Of course, I will. Give me all the information, and we will work it out."

She continues to tell me about calling Beth right after she found out, and also telling her parents. I remember them being nice people, but her dad seemed overprotective. I'm surprised he didn't lecture her or toss her out when she told them. Instead, she told me he gave her a big hug and told her things have a way of working out. God, I hope he's right. Right now, I can't seem to find the open door.

We say our goodbyes, and I get ready for the day and to tell my parents how they are going to be grandparents sooner than we thought. I know Mom is going to be over the moon. She's wanted me to give her a grandbaby since she got sick. I just don't want to break her heart if she's not able to see the baby as often as she would like.

I wonder if I were to ask her to marry me, what would she say? I want her with me so bad it hurts. I don't want to spend more time apart from her than I need to. Before heading over to the ranch, I want to stop at the jewelry store and price rings. I wonder if I made the grand gesture, and went out there with a ring and a promise, would she agree to be mine so we can do this right?

My mind whirls with options and how we can make this work. I'm sure there's a way I can keep the ranch running and find a new job out in Boston. I have my degree in business, and I've been running my own business for years now. I could do city life, right? I sigh heavily, thinking about my few days in the city. It was fun being with Lana, but the noise drove me insane. I wonder if she would be open to moving into more of the suburbs, a compromise of sorts?

I never knew there were so many options when it comes to picking out a damned ring. Cut, carat, style, price, it's almost overwhelming. The older man behind the counter approaches me to offer his assistance. I give him a general idea as to what I'm looking for and tell him a little bit about Lana, per his request. His smile is genuine as I talk about her and the things I love about her.

He pulls out a few rings, and as soon as he shows me a round solitaire diamond set in white gold, I know that's the one. It's perfect. I can picture her wearing it and showing it off to friends and family. On a whim, I purchase it and tuck the box into my pocket for safekeeping. No one needs to know about this yet, not until I know she's really willing to be mine forever.

Except that's not what happens. Holden is waiting for me with a big goofy grin on his face.

"What are you smiling about?" I mutter as I push past him, my good mood slightly soured by his expression.

"What were you doing in the ring shop this morning?"

"What were you doing in town?" I counter.

"Leaving a date's house to come here. Don't try to avoid my question." He snickers when I snarl at him.

"I want to do things right with Lana. We've done everything ass-backward. The one thing I can do right is this. She's carrying my kid. I want to be with her, and what better way than to get hitched and tie her down?"

He chuckles. "Didn't know she was that kinky. Maybe I should have tried to hook up with her years ago."

"Watch it," I warn.

He puts his hands up in surrender and walks away, whistling to himself. Mom and Dad come outside, and I try to act nonchalant. Too bad my parents know me better than that. I pull them back into the house because this is not a conversation we need to have in front of guests.

I sit them down at the breakfast nook and tell them Lana's pregnant. I watch a whirlwind of emotions flash across both their faces. My dad settles into disbelief, and my mom's eyes shine with unshed tears. I don't have the heart to tell her Lana and the baby probably aren't moving out here and that I'm most likely going to give up the ranch to be with her. Now isn't the time. I want the two of them to enjoy this moment.

"How far along is she?" Mom asks.

"Early. About eight weeks is what she told me. Her first

ultrasound is next week, so I am going to be there for it. I want to be there for her in whatever way she'll let me."

Both my parents give me a hug, but Mom drags me away to her bedroom so we can have a private conversation.

"I've always liked that girl, Tristan. She's good for you. You're different around her. I don't care how this baby came to be; I just want you to do the right thing and ask her to marry you." I try to tell her I'm already planning on it when she holds up her hand to stop me. "It doesn't have to happen right away. I want to know you're happy. I don't know how much longer I'll be around, and I need to know you and your father are going to be taken care of."

"Mom, don't talk like that. You're on the mend. The doctors said things look good."

She offers me a smile, but it doesn't reach her eyes. "I know what the doctors have said, but listen to what I'm telling you. I've been sick long enough to know the importance of finding what makes you happy. I know you're happy here on the ranch, but it's only half your life. You need someone to share it with."

She opens her jewelry box and hands me a small ring. The diamond isn't as big as the one I bought Lana, but it isn't any less beautiful. The design has a vintage flair to it, with the intricate design of the metal.

"This was my grandmother's, and I always hoped to have a child I could pass it down to. I want you to use this ring to ask Lana to be your wife." She places it in my hand and closes my fingers around it. "Please, do this for me, Tristan."

I'm not sure what I can say, so I don't say anything and just nod instead. I uncurl my fingers and hold the delicate ring between my thumb and forefinger, examining it. I thought the ring I bought today was perfect, but this one? This one is outstanding. It is Lana. It's delicate, beautiful, and has just enough sparkle to not be overbearing.

CHAPTER 21

LANA

$\mathcal{I}$ stare at Eloise's office. Her nameplate on the wall to the side taunts me as I attempt to gather my thoughts and courage to tell her what I need. There are a few people in cubes around me, each involved in private conversations, and when I hear a lull, I know they're staring at me. I don't want to look like a crazy girl in the office, so I finally knock and wait for her to tell me to come in.

I close the door behind me again and take the seat opposite her. She pulls her glasses down her nose and places them on her desk.

"What can I do for you, Lana?" she asks. I look around her office, taking everything in. This office screams Eloise and sophistication. The white walls harbor a few abstract pictures in different shades of white, gold, and silver. She has a vase of fresh flowers that offer a splash of color. "Lana?" she asks again as I drag my eyes up to meet hers.

"I'm pregnant," I blurt out.

She pulls back, clearly not expecting that to be what I'm here to tell her, and then it's like the flood gates open, and I can't contain it. She's always been a confidant here. Never judging me, and always willing to lend an ear. She has no idea how thankful I am for that.

I tell her my past with the ranch and with Tristan. I tell her how we've been rekindling since she sent me away on this project, and how everything is falling apart.

"Are you happy about this?"

I take a minute to really think about it, and the more I do, the more I want the nine months to be over to meet the little guy. I nod and blink away the tears that have formed.

She stands, walks around her desk, and pulls me in for a hug. "Then I'm very happy for you, Lana. Don't let opportunities pass you by because you're afraid." She motions for me to sit, and I sink down, happy to get off my shaking legs. "Did I ever tell you I lost love once, in favor of a job?"

I shake my head, and when she smiles at me, I know she's happy to tell me.

"I've been around for some time now, and I've seen a lot in my day. Let me tell you, no job is worth it if you can't be with someone who makes you happy. I fell in love with George when we were barely teenagers. I knew he was the one I wanted to be with, even if he didn't know it. We never dated in school, but our paths often crossed through our careers."

I scrunch my brows. I don't want to interrupt her, but when she sees the confusion written on my face, she chimes in.

"Yes, George is now my husband, but we could have been together for a lot longer if we weren't scared."

She continues to tell me how they each found jobs in different cities, and fate happened to bring them together again one weekend, years later. They were both working at architecture firms; she was in Boston, and he was in Philadelphia. The client wanted a meeting with both companies and flew them to New York for the meeting.

Her room got booked next to his, and one drink led to two, and two led to her going back to his room. The only thing keeping them apart was the distance. They struggled with it for a few months before finally ending their relationship. They both moved on, formed new relationships, but in the end, they couldn't be without one another. He moved up to Boston, and they started the company together.

It really is a great story. I had no idea she and George took so long to come together. Anytime I've seen them together at the office or a company outing, he worships her. "Thank you for sharing that with me."

"All I'm saying is, don't be afraid to do what makes you happy. Things have a way of working out."

"I'll take that to heart."

I leave her office feeling better than I have since I found out about the baby.

Tristan arrives today, and I'm nervous as I stand by baggage claim at Logan Airport, which is bustling with travelers. I watch an elderly couple reunite in a flurry of hugs and kisses. He's holding a bouquet of flowers for her even though he's the one who was traveling. It warms my heart, knowing they are so in love.

I stand at the foot of the escalator and look at my phone. No calls, no texts, and he should have landed fifteen minutes ago. I'm starting to get nervous that he didn't make his flight and won't be here. The ultrasound is in a few hours, and I can't be late for it. When I look back up, I see him coming down. He looks amazing in a snug t-shirt, dark wash jeans, and boots. *He could pull me into the bathroom and have his way with me, and I'd be okay with that.*

Damn hormones. Or maybe it's not hormones, but he just looks that good. I look around and see a few other girls looking his way and smiling. Something inside me snaps when I see them ogling him, and I make a dash for him as he steps off the escalator. He sees me coming toward him, and he drops his bag and scoops me up, spinning me around in his arms.

"I've missed you so damn much, baby," he murmurs into the crook of my neck before placing me on my feet again. I reach up and touch my lips to his, keeping it brief but no less sinful.

"I've missed you, too. I'm glad you could come for this." I intertwine my fingers through his and pull him along the path to my car in the garage.

"I wouldn't miss this for the world, Lana. I told you I want to be a part of our kid's life. I don't want him or her to grow up without a father."

I ask him about his flight and how the build is going as I think about what he said. He wants to be part of their life. I want that more than anything, and I know how happy he is at the ranch. I can't picture him living here in the city—he'd be miserable. When he's packing stuff in my car, it's then I notice a garment bag.

"Tristan, what's in the bag?"

His face reddens, and he smirks as he looks to his feet. "I thought I'd look for a job in Boston. I have an interview while I'm here."

"*What?*" I yell on a shriek. The look of panic on his face has me retracting my statement. "No, no, I don't mean it in a bad way, I'm just surprised is all. What about the ranch? Your family?"

"I told Mom and Dad what's going on and how I feel about you and this baby. I want to make things work, and I don't want you to sacrifice your home and job in order to do so." He shrugs like he is telling me about the weather. "So, I applied for a few jobs and have an interview."

I'm in shock. I'm driving on auto-pilot, watching the white-lined road in front of me but not really focusing on where I'm going.

When I don't respond, he continues. "Are you mad?"

"N-no." I take a deep breath and release it slowly. "No. I'm not mad." How do I put this in words? How do I tell him I don't want him giving up his life and his dream at the ranch for me? I'm not worth that. I'm not worth him potentially being unhappy living somewhere else. "I don't want you to regret your decisions. That's all."

I don't want him to think he's happy and have things fall apart. We already have a lot to work on, and I don't need him doing anything rash to try to fix things. The thought that he's willing to give up his life back home for me warms my heart. That's a big decision, and even if he hasn't thought it through all the way, it's still a nice gesture.

We get to the apartment, and I help him get his things inside. I stand in the doorway of my room and watch the muscles in his back flex under his shirt as he moves around my space as if he owns it. I lick my lips, unable to contain the sexy memories running through my mind. He glances over at me and smirks. As if he can read my mind, he pulls his shirt over his head and drops it on the floor next to him.

"Does my cowgirl need a ride?"

My eyes must be the size of saucers as I bite my lip. He unbuttons his jeans, slowly pulls the zipper, and drags them down his legs. He sits at the edge of the bed in just his boxer briefs, and I drop to my knees in front of him, desperate to feel and taste him. I pull at the waistband and reach my hand in, grasping his length and giving him a few strokes.

He pulls at my shirt, and I release him long enough for him

to pull it over my head. He tosses it on the floor on top of his. I go back to work, gripping his hard cock, and wrap my lips around him. He leans his weight back on his hands and drops his head on a moan when I swirl my tongue around the tip.

"Fuck, Lana. That feels so nice. I love when you suck me. You're so fucking good at it."

His praise pushes me a little closer to my own edge. I'm soaked after a few minutes of the moans and praise filling the space between us. He pulls me off him when I start to feel him pulsing in my mouth, and I pout. He stands, pulling me up with him, and molds my body against his as he plants a searing kiss on my lips and neck. His kisses move lower as his fingers fumble to push my pants out of the way. I reach behind me, helping him unclasp my bra. When my breasts fall free, I wince, and it doesn't go unnoticed.

"They're tender. Just be gentle with them."

He nods and pulls me on the bed with him. He lies on his back, legs spread, and I climb on top of him. He helps line me up, and I slide down, taking him in, inch by glorious inch. We moan in unison. This feels like home. It's what I needed, and it's where he belongs. That's a scary thought, so I push it from my mind and work on enjoying him, enjoying us.

He lies back, letting me use him to work myself over. I rock back and forth, using his pelvis to add the extra stimulation to my clit. I could sit up here all day just to feel him buried deep inside me. There is nothing better, and he knows what he's doing. I picture all the ways I want him to take me and come undone after a few minutes.

He puts me on my hands and knees and presses in from behind me. I lower my chest to the bed, letting him work in as deep as he can get.

"Jesus, Lana, you're so fucking beautiful." He sets a steady rhythm and, with easy thrusts, pushes me forward a bit. God, I need to feel owned right now. I need to feel like we belong to each other. I rest my cheek on the bed, put both my hands on my lower back, and let him take over.

He wraps his large hands around my wrists, holding them in place as he slaps my ass and takes me faster. An unexpected orgasm rips through me, and I moan and pant into the comforter as he follows suit and comes deep inside me.

Heaven.

That's the only way I'd describe being with him. He knows my body so well. He knows my likes and dislikes, and he knows not to be selfish. I can't let him move out here for me. I think of the story Eloise told me about her and George and how I shouldn't be afraid. I can see myself living on that ranch, being there with Tristan and his family. Raising our child in a simpler part of the country where he or she can have the experiences that aren't available around here.

I want to move to Wyoming with Tristan and make this work with him. I don't want him giving up everything to be here in Boston. He would hate it, and I would be miserable because he was.

I feel lighter than I have in weeks, and I want to tell him before he wastes his time going on the interview. Tonight at dinner will be perfect. I have the whole thing planned in my head. We will go to the ultrasound, get excited to see the heartbeat and such, then I will suggest we go out to dinner to celebrate. Of course, he will say yes, and then I will tell him during dessert.

I'm giddy as I plan this in my head. I'm trying to keep my expression neutral because I don't want to tip him off.

Tristan Ellis, you and I will finally get our chance.

CHAPTER 22

TRISTAN

*L*ana's up on the table with the paper sheet over her lap when the sonographer comes back. The room's lights are dim, and it smells like a hospital. Sterile. Lana takes in a deep breath as the woman presses what looks like a probe into her. I scoot the chair a little closer to the padded table and hold her hand in mine. She glances at me with a huge smile on her face and then focuses on the black and white screen in front of her.

"There's your baby's heartbeat," the woman says, pointing to the small fluttering on the screen.

I'm floored as I watch. That's my baby in there. Lana is going to be the mother of our child. She continues to speak, talking about the size of the baby and the progression. I'm not sure how she's able to make out anything on that screen. It just looks like a bunch of black blobs to me, but if she tells me there's a baby there, then there is.

"Do you want some pictures?"

"Yes," I blurt out before Lana can speak.

She smiles at me and looks at the sonographer again. "Please, thank you so much."

I can hardly contain my excitement when she hands the small photos over. "Can I take a picture to send to my parents?"

She nods, and I snap one real quick and send the text to both of them.

"Everything is looking great. We'll have to meet with the nurse to go over the next steps with you."

She leaves, and Lana gets her pants back on. "Wow, it's crazy, huh? I mean, I don't look any different, and I don't feel too different, but there it is. Baby Ellis."

My head snaps up to look at her, and her smile is infectious. Baby Ellis. I like that. I'll like it even better if she decides to be Mrs. Lana Ellis. I pat my pocket where my mother's ring is nestled in a box for safekeeping. I've been paranoid about losing it all day, especially when she all but attacked me at her apartment.

We are ushered into another exam room and wait for the nurse to come in and see us. I can tell she's excited but a little anxious as well. She keeps playing with her fingers and the bottom of her shirt. I reach over, take her hand in mine, and kiss the back of her knuckles.

"It's going to be fine. She said everything looks great. There's nothing to be concerned about."

Lana nods and gives me a smile that warms me from head to toe. I can't stop looking at her.

"You know, you keep looking at me like that, we won't make it out of this room," she jokes, but I can tell she's actually quite serious.

The nurse comes in and tells us all about the ultrasound. What we were looking at and how far along she is. She's a little under ten weeks, which means she probably got pregnant one of the first times we slept together. *Damn*. If this isn't fate pushing us together, I don't know what is.

The nurse hands her a stack of papers and a list of dos and don'ts while pregnant. We stop at the checkout desk and set up all her appointments until the end of her pregnancy. My heart sinks a little. I know she's staying here, and I know I'm going to look for a job out here to be close to her, but I kind of hoped she would tell them she wouldn't need it because she's moving. A small part of me hoped she would say something like that, but I knew that wasn't going to happen.

I have an interview tomorrow in downtown Boston at the Prudential Center, and I hope it works out. It's for an entry-level project manager position. I feel too damn old to be taking an entry-level position, but since I've only had the ranch experience, I figured it was safer to start lower in hopes someone would recommend me for a higher position. I could work my way through the ranks quickly.

"I'm starving. Want to go to dinner?" she asks as we step into the parking garage.

I smile. "Sure, what are you in the mood for?"

"Little Italy in the north end isn't too far from here. Want some amazing pasta and then a cannoli from *Mike's Pastry* around the corner?"

"Sounds great. Bring me to your favorite spot. I want to treat my girl to dinner tonight."

She claps her hands and starts the car, pulling out into the business traffic in downtown Boston. I have no idea how she can navigate through the throng of vehicles. I have no problem driving and can off-road with the best of them, but put me here and tell me I have to drive in it all the time, and I might want to chop my head off. Horns blare from every which direction, and I have no idea who they are honking at.

It doesn't even seem to faze her as she looks in her side mirror and cuts over into the turn lane with ease.

"Do you always drive through the city?"

"Not usually. I take the T more often because it's easier, but for today, I didn't want to be late or have to arrive wicked early."

I narrow my eyes in confusion at her. "Wicked?"

She smirks, and a light pink blush creeps up her neck. "There are a few things I've picked up from living around here, and *wicked* is one of them."

The restaurant is a few blocks from the parking garage she pulls into. As soon as I round the corner, I take her hand in mine. She wraps her other hand around my upper arm and leans her head against me for the briefest of moments. We really look like a happy little family. I tap the box again in my pocket and smile.

Soon.

Dinner is everything she said it would be and more. She insisted I order a drink even though she couldn't have anything, and I'm thankful for the liquid courage. As the night wears on, the damned box is burning a hole in my pocket. I want this to be perfect—it has to be perfect. I want her to remember everything about this moment. I want to get home and ask her to marry me in a place where she can be loud, cry, or act like her goofy, adorable self.

I pay the bill, and we walk to the pastry around the corner, right where she said it was. The line is long and around the corner, but we wait patiently. It moves a lot faster than I would have expected, the workers experienced enough to keep it moving at a good clip. People keep walking out with huge smiles and the same white box.

As soon as we enter the doors, my senses are assaulted with sugary sweets and noise from all the people in the confined space. There are what appear to be hundreds of treats behind the glass containers, and I want to sample a little of everything.

We finally reach the front, and she orders a box of six cannolis, a dozen Italian cookies, and some macaroons. The guy behind the counter hands her a bright white box with a blue logo and a blue and white striped string tied in a bow. I have no idea where she's going to pack them away. There are no spots to sit, so we walk back to her car to get to her apartment to eat our tasty treats.

I carry the pastry box up the stairs and hold her hand the entire way home, afraid she will disappear on me if I don't. I put it down on the counter, and she pulls out plates for us. She comes back, unties the string, and pops the top on the box.

"Enjoy," she announces as she takes a fresh cannoli.

Let me tell you, these treats are nothing like what I get at home. Not that I eat many cannolis, but these are still the best ones I've ever eaten. Her small moans of approval indicate just how much she likes her treat.

"So, I have something I want to talk to you about," she says.

I put my dessert down and wipe my hands and mouth on a napkin. "Okay," I state.

She looks worried. That doesn't bode well for me, and I try to keep my emotions in check as she gathers the courage to say whatever she's thinking. Time ticks by so slowly. I reach my hand across the table, enveloping her small one in mine, giving her a reassuring squeeze.

"What would you say about me moving out to Wyoming?" I stare at her in disbelief. *Did I hear her right? She wants to move for me?* "Someone recently told me a story about not letting chances slip by, and I really think this is sort of a sign. You came back into my life, and we are having this baby for a reason."

My mouth flops like a fish as I compose my thoughts. Right

now, I want to squeeze her as hard as I can, spin her around, and never let her go. I need to be rational about this. I don't want her rushing into anything and then regretting her decision. I mean, I'm going to ask her to marry me, but I figured I'd be moving for her.

"Say something," she whispers as she plays with the hem of her shirt and tucks some hair behind her ear.

I still don't know what to say. I'm dumbfounded she would alter her life so much to be with me—of all people. "Baby, are you sure?" I finally ask. The look on her face is one of pure dread. I hold her cheeks between my hands and rub my thumbs over her smooth skin. "Nothing would make me happier than if you would move out to Wyoming so we can make this work between us. I want to be a part of your life and our child's."

"Really?" she asks, her face lighting up.

How can she really ask that? Does she not understand I'd move Heaven and Earth for her?

"Lana, I've wanted you with me since I was dumb enough to push you away. I want to make sure you're positive about this. I don't want you to think you're the only one who is giving up something to make this work. I'm happy to move out to Boston and find a job here, so you don't have to give up your career, family, and friends. I don't want you to hate me in the future if you do this."

"I want to do this, Tristan. There are other jobs. Things have a way of working out. Maybe Eloise will let me stay on and work remotely. If not, maybe I will try to start my own firm and work with some of the businesses in the area."

I pull her lips to mine, showing her exactly how much this means to me. The kiss starts off sweet at first but quickly morphs into a steamy, passion-filled one. I taste the pastry on her lips and tongue—so sweet. She's perfect. Everything about Lana Robinson is perfect. Everything is right with the world.

I pull away, pull the ring box from my pocket, and slide down to one knee. I open the box, and she gasps at my mother's vintage ring staring back at her. She covers her mouth with her fingers and blinks away tears.

"Lana, you mean everything to me. Fate has brought you back to me, and only a real fool would be stupid enough to let you go again. I'm sorry for what happened between us in the past, but we can't change that now. We can only look to the future, and you're my future. I want to spend the rest of my life showing you exactly how much you mean to me. Will you marry me?"

CHAPTER 23

LANA

I stare at him, not sure I heard the words coming out correctly. *Will you marry me?* He shifts his weight around as he waits for my answer. The longer it takes, the more he's starting to sweat. I have to put the poor guy out of his misery.

"Are you sure?" I bite my lower lip, waiting.

"You're the only thing in my whole damn life I've ever been sure of."

"Yes, Tristan." I nod my head vigorously to drive home my answer. Tears prick my eyes as I push the words past my lips. "I'll marry you."

He slips the beautiful ring on my finger and scoops me up in his arms, pressing his lips to mine. It's a perfect moment. He sets me on my feet but keeps his hands on my hips. I hold my left hand in front of me and admire the ornate ring.

"Where did you find this? It's perfect, exactly the ring I've always wanted," I gush.

"Mom gave it to me."

I jerk my head up to look into his eyes. "Your parents knew you were going to ask me?"

He nods. "Mom is thrilled. They also both know about the baby, too."

"You said your mom is thrilled. Is your dad not happy?" I play with the bottom of my shirt as I wait for him to respond.

"He wants what's best for me. I think he's afraid I'll give up the ranch and we'll have to close it down. He knows you make me happy, and he's thrilled to be a grandfather.

"Come on, let's get you to bed. We have a lot of planning to do for the few days I'm here. I'll help in any way I can. I don't want you rushing into anything, so if you want to stay here until you deliver, that's fine with me. I'll be here any way I can." We walk to the bedroom and change into pajamas before crawling into bed.

Wow, I didn't even think of that. I spent all this time picking out the perfect doctor for my little nugget, yet as soon as Tristan told me he was looking for a job, I was ready to change my life around in a flash for him.

I really am in too deep.

"I want to talk with Eloise, and I haven't decided on where I want to give birth. I really want you here with me for all the steps, but I know that won't be possible right now. It's still early in the pregnancy, so I have a little bit of time to figure it out." I hesitate. "I want to bring you home to my parents. They remember you from our trip, and I think it would be good for them to see the man you have become."

He takes a deep breath and nods. "I'd love to do that." He smiles, but it's not quite as genuine as I'd hope.

"What's wrong? You don't like my parents?"

He shakes his head. "It's not that. I'm the asshole that knocked up their only daughter. I don't imagine they're going to be thrilled to see me."

I toss my leg over his hip and turn him on his side so he's facing me. "You're also the man that is trying to make it right and wants to be there. Not everyone would do that." He nods, and I snuggle down into him.

"I saw you graduate, you know?" he says. I'm almost asleep and nearly miss it. I sit up and look down at him in shock. "I was planning on seeing you and sweeping you off your feet, but I saw how well you were doing without me. I didn't want to ruin anything for you." He tucks some loose hair behind my ear.

My lips turn up in a small smirk. "I knew you were there. I didn't see you, but I could feel you. Beth thought I was crazy. I'm glad you didn't talk to me, though, as much as I hate to admit it. I was finally in a decent headspace, and seeing you would have brought it all rushing back."

"I couldn't do that to you. I didn't want to cause you any more heartache than I already did." He kisses the top of my head, and I fall asleep to the sound of his steady heartbeat.

One thing at a time. I want him to see my parents and talk to them before I give Eloise my notice. I need them to be able to accept the decisions I'm about to make. I need their love and support through this. I know, in the grand scheme of things, it doesn't matter, but I want everyone to get along.

I pull up outside their house in Connecticut, and we get out. He's in his dark dress slacks and a button-down top. The top two buttons are left open, and if that doesn't add to his sexiness, I don't know what will. His shoes are shined nicely. I don't think I've ever seen him look so professional.

"You clean up nice," I say, taking his hand in mine as we walk up the front steps.

He smirks. "You make it seem like I don't know how to dress nicely. Although, I thought you preferred me in my cowboy get up."

"Oh, I do, but this might tie for first place."

I push open the front door and call out for Mom and Dad. They are sitting in the living room and get up to meet us as we step into the foyer. I give them each a hug as Tristan shakes Dad's hand, but Mom pulls him down for a hug.

"Wow, he's very handsome, isn't he?" Mom whispers to me.

"Yes, he is. Don't embarrass me."

I had taken my ring off before we walked inside. I want to talk to them first before I spring the fact we are getting married to them. Tristan has already told me we can do it at the ranch if we want, and it wouldn't cost a lot to do so. He said he doesn't care where it happens, just as long as he can finally call me his. *If that's not book-worthy, I don't know what is.*

We sit down at the table after each of us grabs a drink, and Mom brings dinner over. Dad jumps right in and starts grilling Tristan about his schooling, the ranch, and even about how he skipped out on me years ago. Tristan handles it all with good grace. I hold his hand under the table and step in a few times when he seems to be struggling.

"So, you're having a baby with my daughter. Are you planning on moving?" he asks.

"Actually, Dad, I'm moving to Wyoming." He stops midbite and puts his fork down. "I've already talked with my boss, and she's agreed to let me work remotely and fly out as needed." *Lies, but he doesn't know.* "The ranch is very important to Tristan and his family, and I don't want him to uproot his life."

"But you're willing to do that for him?" he questions.

"Yes." I pull the ring from my purse and slip it on to my finger. "He's asked me to marry him, and I've accepted. He's a good man, Dad. I love him, and he's who I want."

Dad glares at Tristan. I'm about to step in again when he starts to talk. "I know my past actions don't put me high on your list of approved people for Lana, but I can promise you, no one will love your daughter like I will. I come from a good family with a strong work ethic. I will work as hard as I can to make sure your daughter and our child have everything they need. I want her and our baby to be happy."

Mom puts her hand on my dad's forearm. "Henry." He looks at her, and his gaze softens. I remember hearing stories about how my Grandpa didn't care for Dad when he met the family, but Dad proved him wrong time and time again.

He sighs, pats my mom's hand, and looks at us. "Are you sure?"

"Yeah, one-hundred percent."

"Do your parents approve, Tristan?"

He glances at me with a huge smile on his face. "My parents love her. You both did a fine job raising her. The ring I gave her was actually my mother's. She gave it to me when I told her I wanted to ask her."

Mom is crying and comes over to give us both a huge hug. She starts asking questions about the wedding—where it will be, when it will be, where we plan on taking a honeymoon. All the standard questions. I wish I could answer them, but I just don't know.

I also don't want anything over the top. I have Tristan; that's enough for me. It's funny how our tastes change from when we are young. When I was little, I wanted an over the top wedding with the biggest dress, the nicest flowers, and the most expensive venue. I wanted to be a princess in every aspect of the word.

Now, I just want to be with Tristan.

First things first, I suppose. I need to speak with Eloise about staying on as a remote worker, and I need to decide if the baby will be born in Massachusetts or Wyoming. *God, help me!*

I leave Tristan in my apartment and walk to the office to meet with Eloise the next morning. When I step into the office, everyone's in a frenzy.

"Hannah, what's going on?" I ask when she gets off the phone.

She holds a magazine out for me to take, and I see a picture of the room I decorated for Mrs. Carrington on it. "Turns out, you're a hit. The phones have been ringing off the hook with people looking to have their houses remodeled, too. We have people in the U.K., along with people across the States. You're an overnight sensation."

I stare in awe at the cover of the magazine. I pull up a message to Russ.

Me: *Tell your mom I said thank you for the magazine.*

Russ: *That's all you, but I will tell her. Congratulations.*

I sit at my desk and read his text over and over. I feel like I should tell him I'm pregnant—that I'm happy—but I can't get myself to do it. The phone on my desk rings, and Eloise is on the other end. She requests me in her office for a chat. I pull myself together and get ready to tell her my news.

I knock and slink in through her doorway. Before I can even sit, she's talking a hundred miles an hour about new projects, clients, and more opportunities to travel. It's everything I had ever wanted and more—except, now I don't.

"Eloise, I'm moving," I say. She stops her buzzing about and looks at me, blinking in surprise.

"What do you mean, you're moving?"

I hold up my hand to show her the ring. "Tristan and I are

going to get married, and I'm moving out to Wyoming. I wanted to talk to you about the chance to stay on remotely. I really enjoy working for this firm, and I have learned a lot in the past year here. I understand if this is not something you will allow, but I didn't want to leave without asking."

She sits and studies me as she contemplates her response. "Lana, are you happy? Does he make you happy?" I smile and nod in response. "Good. I'm glad to see you took my conversation to heart."

"I did. This feels right. He was put back in my path for a reason. I need to be able to explore this with him."

She nods, and a sweet smile graces her lips. "I'm glad. Now, about you working remotely." I hold my breath, waiting for her to give me her final decision. "What are the chances you could fly out here once a month for a few days, just to have some presence in the office?"

I can hardly contain my excitement. I want to pump my fists in the air *Breakfast Club* style, but I bite the inside of my cheek and smile wide. "I'm sure I could make that work."

"Perfect. Then I don't see why this can't work. You have a lot of people who are contacting us to work with you directly. You'll have first pick of the projects and where they're located."

She continues to talk, but I don't hear any of it. I am too excited about the fact that everything seems to be coming together for us. I'll move out there, oversee the cabin project, get married, have a baby, and live happily ever after.

Right?

God, I really hope I'm making the right choice. Everything is happening so fast that I feel I'm not in control of it. What I really need is to go home and sort everything out with my landlord, and with Tristan. Please, let the rest of the day go by fast.

CHAPTER 24

TRISTAN - SIX MONTHS LATER

I carry the last of her boxes into my apartment, and as I look around, I know we need to find something bigger. Our baby will be here in a month, and this one-bedroom apartment is way too small. I didn't want to go looking for a place without her. I have some money in savings, and my plan is to go house shopping with her. He or she is going to need room to run around.

Lana decided she wanted to finish out her prenatal care in Boston, and it's been hard on us but so worth it. She's out here this week to do a final walk-through of the cabins. She will then return home until she has the baby and then move out this way. She's been sending stuff over a little at a time, and she is down to bare minimums. It's so exciting. I can't wait until she's here full time. This distance thing is torture.

"Babe, I was thinking, would you want to look for a bigger place this week?"

She takes a deep breath, her round stomach sticking out in the most adorable manner. "Sure." She struggles to stand from her spot on the couch, and when I try to help her, she swats my hand away. "I'm a strong, independent woman," she teases.

"Yes, you are, but I want to spoil you, so let me. I haven't seen you in a month, and I've missed you." She stands in front of me, her belly pressing into me as she stands on her tip-toes and kisses me. *God, I've missed these kisses.* Three more months and she will be out here with me for good. Three more months until we can be a full-time family.

We set a wedding date for next year, so the baby will be about a year old and can be either the flower girl or ring bearer. We haven't found out what we're having yet. She wants it to be a surprise, and it's driving me insane. Every time I mention calling the doctor to find out, she gets this twinkle in her eye. She's up to something, but I don't know what it is.

The ride to the ranch takes longer than it should because some of the dirt road has potholes, and I don't want to jostle her too much. I did promise to take her out into the field to see the horses today after she does her final check-in and signs off on it all.

She slides out of the truck, and my mom comes out the front door to greet us with a large smile and hug for Lana.

"Lana, honey, you look great. So happy to have you back here," she says, kissing her on the cheek.

"Hi, Liz, it's good to be home."

Home. That's the first time I've heard her say it, and as if she knew, she turns to look at me. The smile on my face matches hers—large and full of love.

I can't wait to have her any longer. "Lana, why don't we take a walk to see the cabins?"

She talks with mom for a few more minutes before we start in the direction of the new building, but I don't stop. I keep pulling her with me until we reach cabin seven. Her eyes sparkle, and she sees the mischief behind mine. She knows what I'm up to; she doesn't even have to ask. I push open the door to the cabin and lock it behind me.

She walks in the direction of the bedroom she slept in when she stayed all those years ago, pulling her shirt over her head as she goes. She looks so fucking beautiful with her stomach round, carrying my child. I follow her into the room just as she kicks her shoes off and is undoing her shorts.

"We gotta make this fast. I want to finish with the project so we can spend more time together," she says as she crawls on the bed on her hands and knees.

I strip down as fast as I can and press into her from behind. She pushes back on me, taking me all the way in.

"Oh, God," she moans.

I slap her ass, and she starts moving as I reach my hand around her to play with her clit. She bucks under my touch, and it's not long before she is breathing heavy and panting for more.

"Come on, baby. Beg for it," I urge, pressing a little harder.

"P-please, Tristan. Please, help me come," she mewls. It's like music to my fucking ears.

"Fuck yourself on me. Take it," I demand.

She moves faster, back and forth over my hard length. I feel myself building from the base of my spine, but I hold off, wanting her to finish before me. A few more well-timed thrusts, and she comes around me, burying her face on the bed, taking everything I have to give her.

We lie together on our sides, spooning as both our heart rates slow down.

"You know, we won't be able to do this in another week." She turns her head to look at me in question. I place my hands over her belly and rub it gently. "This cabin, along with the new ones, are rented out for the rest of the year, and they're eighty-percent full for a few months after that."

"Oh my God, Tristan, that's amazing!" She pulls my face to hers, giving me an excited kiss. "You've been working so hard here. I'm so happy for you." She takes a deep breath, and her eyes go wide. "Did you feel that?"

I shake my head, and she moves my hand to where the baby just kicked. It does it again, and I'm in awe. I climb over her so I'm in front of her stomach and press my hand over the little hand that presses against her belly.

"He likes that daddy's close," she says on a whisper.

I'm smiling, unable to contain my excitement. "Yeah, I guess so." *Wait, did she just say he?* I look into her bright eyes, and she nods. "We're having a boy? You found out without me?"

"I didn't mean to. The nurse slipped when we were talking, but yeah, we're having a boy, Tristan." She starts to cry, and I pull her to me. "Gah, stupid hormones, I can't get this emotional."

When I try to ask her when she found out, she curls into herself and takes a few deep breaths in through her nose and out through her mouth. She continues until her body relaxes.

"Lana, babe, you okay?"

She tries to offer me a smile, but it looks pained. "I'm fine. He's just being a brat."

A few minutes later, she curls into herself again, and this time grunts with the pain. What the hell did I read? Pre-labor contractions are about five minutes apart? I look at the clock and see it's been about that time.

"Lana, I think you're going into labor." I help her sit up, and she curls over her stomach, trying to help the ache.

She shakes her head and squeezes her eyes shut. "Not possible. I'm not due for another month." She stands to get her clothes, and water runs down her legs in a steady stream. She looks at me with horror in her eyes. "Tristan, I'm not due yet."

"Well, he has other plans. Come on, let's get you to the hospital."

I help her into some clothes and up into the truck. The closest hospital is about twenty minutes away. My palms are sweaty as I grip the steering wheel, trying to remember how to get to the hospital in my state of panic. She reaches over and places her hand on my thigh, and it's like she takes some of the anxiety away from a simple touch.

"It's going to be fine, Tristan."

I take her hand in mine and lift it to my lips, planting a kiss on the back of her knuckles. I'm trying my damndest not to crash, especially when she doubles over in pain and groans through her breathing.

"This wasn't the plan," she groans through gritted teeth.

"I know, baby, but it looks like he's got his own plan. We're almost there."

I pull up to the emergency room doors and jump out to help her. We walk through the sliding doors, and hospital staff has her sit as I fill them in on what's going on. A nurse wheels her away and tells me they'll get her in a room while I go move the truck. Someone must be looking out for me because I see an open spot immediately.

I throw the truck in park and jog back into the hospital. The nurse behind the counter gives me her room number, and I race down the hall as fast as I can. She's already in a dressing gown and is lying on her side, clutching her stomach.

"Someone do something. She's in pain," I say to the nurses in the room.

One of them glares at me, and the other pats my shoulder. "First time?" I nod at her question. "She's got a while to go. She's only five centimeters dilated. We need her to get to ten before she can start pushing."

The other staff members in the room start hooking her up

to tubes and monitoring devices. I sit next to her bed and offer my hand for her to squeeze whenever the pain hits. I always knew this girl had some strength behind her, but I didn't know just how strong she was. When she releases my fingers, they are purple, and I have to squeeze them a few times for the blood to start flowing again.

How much longer until he's here?

He's perfect, and little, and I'm the happiest man in the entire world. Never in a million years did I think I would feel love this strong for any one human. Lana did so well and is relaxing comfortably in the bed as I hold little William Henry Ellis. God, he really is perfect. He looks so much like me, but he has his mom's nose. I lift him to my face to kiss his perfect skin and inhale his fresh baby scent.

Mom and Dad should be here soon to meet their first grandson. I called Lana's parents, and they have a flight out tomorrow. They will see us when we are discharged from the hospital.

Lana blinks at me and smiles as she watches me cuddle up with the little guy.

"Hey, cowboy," she says, her voice thick with sleep.

"Hey, yourself, Momma."

She holds her arms out for him, and I pass him over. She whispers to him as she feeds him. She's a natural at this. It's second nature to her.

"How did you get so good at this?" I ask, watching in awe.

"Lots of reading and hoping for the best. You'll get there. I've had time to get to know him. You've only just met. Give it a few days, and you'll be a natural."

Mom and Dad show up a short while later and hug and kiss

both of us before giving William lots of love and cuddles. There is no doubt this kid is going to be adored by everyone in the family. They stay for about an hour until Lana finally starts to fall asleep, and I walk them out. I don't want to leave too long, even though the nurses and staff are taking care of him.

"He's adorable, Tristan. I'm so happy for you both," Mom says as she pulls me into a tight embrace.

Dad gives me a few words of encouragement, pulls me into a hug, and claps his hand on my back.

CHAPTER 25

LANA

*M*oving day. I thought it would never get here. I had to take William back to Massachusetts with me so I could finish getting everything in order, and it was tough for Tristan to let us go. He's always been protective of me, but around William, he's a whole different person. He's going to be a good dad to him.

Since Simone had that article printed, I have been receiving offers non-stop for remodeling work, and Eloise has been good about filtering things to me that won't take me too far from home. I'm so thankful to have her in my corner. I'm also lucky she understood when I told her I wanted to branch off and start my own company.

It's time, and she knew it. She has been great at helping me get things up and running so I can work out of the office space in my new house. Eloise has sent a few clients my way to help me out, and I will officially be open for business in another two months. No way I'm rushing through spending time with my little man.

"Babe, you about ready to leave?" Tristan asks as he walks into the empty bedroom.

I have William in my arms as I look around, remembering the times I spent here. I can't believe how much my life has changed in such a short time.

"I can't believe I'm moving out to Wyoming. God, if you would have told me ten years ago our lives would have ended up like this, I would never have believed it."

He smirks and plants a gentle kiss on my lips. "I'm the luckiest man in the world that you were willing to come to me. I know I am, and I want you to know how much I love you and our little man."

I put him down in his car seat as Tristan pulls me against him and drops his lips to mine for a searing kiss. He slides his tongue along the seam of my lips, and I open for him, giving him what he wants. He presses me against the wall, holding my hands above me.

"How much time do you think we have?" he asks, grinding into me.

I gasp and hum my appreciation as his rigid length digs into my stomach. "Probably only five minutes or so. Dad texted me, saying they're close." I press my hips against his as he drops his lips to my neck. "Besides, wouldn't you much rather fuck me in our new bed, which will be in our new home when we arrive in a few hours? It would be much nicer than against a wall."

"Says who? Against the wall is much more fun. It's risky, dirty, and possibly messy." He kisses a trail down my neck to my covered breasts, and as if William can sense his mom and dad are about to have some grown-up fun, he lets out a wail. Tristan and I jump apart, and he scoops him up into his arms.

"Little man, you gotta let Momma and me have a little bit of fun," he chastises the little boy quietly. "Don't you want a baby sister or brother?"

"Hold it right there, buddy. He's more than enough for right now," I say, admiring my two handsome men.

A few more hours and everything will be right.

The flight was long and bumpy. William did well for the first few hours, sleeping through everything, but then he woke up and demanded to be heard. I spent the last two hours of the flight walking up and down the aisles, trying to calm him, and when we weren't walking, I was trying to feed him. Neither worked to calm him.

By the time we landed, he was so exhausted that he slept the whole ride to Grammy and Grampy's. When we told Liz and John we wanted to get William's room set up, they jumped at the chance to watch him. This is going to be the first time he's not with me, and I'm anxious about it.

I give him a million kisses until, finally, he gets annoyed and starts moving his arms around to get away from me.

"Okay, little man, Mom and Dad will see you in the morning," I say, planting one more kiss on his forehead. I hand the diaper bag over to John as Liz holds the baby. "There are bottles in there that need to go in the fridge, and there should be plenty of diapers and clothes for him. Please, call us if you have any problems, and we will come get him right away."

Tristan pulls me to his side and kisses my head. "Babe, he's going to be fine. Stop worrying."

"Lana, he's going to be fine, but if we run into any problems, we will call straight away," Liz says. "Go have fun, you two." She smirks, and I know she knows what's probably going to happen.

Tristan helps me into the truck, and when we pull away, the tears start welling up. I wipe the water under my eyes and try to focus on the road. I can see him watching me from the corner of my eye, and he wraps my hand up in his.

"He's going to be fine. It's just for the night. You will see him bright and early tomorrow," he says, trying to reassure me.

Our new home comes into view, and I smile. It's perfect for us. There's enough land for William to run around, and if we decide to grow our little family, there is extra room or enough space to add an addition. When we bought it, I was thinking a starter home, but now I can see this being a forever home. The best part, too, is it's private. No neighbors for a half a mile and no traffic. It's taken me a while to get used to hearing nature instead of traffic, but I wouldn't change it.

"Now, Mrs. Ellis-to-be, you have been driving me crazy since Boston, and I'm in desperate need of your body pressed under mine. Get your ass into our bedroom and get out of those clothes."

I hesitate and look down at myself. My stomach still sticks out, my thighs and arms are a little more jiggly than they were before, and my hips are wider. Nothing about me looks the same as it did before having William.

He can sense what I'm thinking. "Stop, Lana." I look up at him. "You're beautiful just like you are. I wouldn't change anything about you."

"I don't look the same," I say quietly in protest.

"No, you don't. You look better. You've given me exactly what I've wanted—a family. I couldn't be happier than I am with you. You're beautiful and perfect for me."

"Really?" I ask, the tears starting again.

He holds my head in his hands and wipes the tears away with the pads of his thumbs before dipping down to kiss me on the lips. Being held in his strong arms is everything I need. My libido thrums alive, and I'm panting before long.

"Get naked, baby. I'll be there in a few minutes." He taps

my butt and sends me on my way to the bedroom where I do as he asks.

We were experimenting with different things in the bedroom before William was born, and I learned how much I enjoy dirty talk and being spanked. He's always been good at talking dirty in the bedroom, but since he knows how much I like it, he's revved up his game.

He saunters in a few minutes later, and I'm standing naked in the middle of the room, waiting for him. I watch as he walks around me like I'm his prey, trying to decide how best to attack.

"You make me so hard, Lana. I want to push you over the side of the bed and shove my cock so deep into you," he says. I moan as my eyes flutter closed. His hand skims over my stomach, and I tense up. "Relax," he demands in my ear. "You're beautiful."

I know better than to dismiss his comment, so I don't say anything. He wraps his fingers around my throat, pulling my face to his for a panty-dropping kiss. *God, this man pushes all the right buttons for me.* I place my hands on his shirt and slide my fingers under it, helping him take it off. I trail my fingers over the roped cords of muscle in his arms and get wetter as I explore.

I slink down on to the plush, cream-colored carpet under my knees and quickly undo his pants, pushing them down his legs. I do the same with his boxers and take his hard cock between my fingers. It's silky and heavy in my grasp, and I glance up at him to see exactly the effect I have on him—talk about a morale booster. His eyelids are heavy, and his head is dropped back the slightest amount.

"Lick it, Lana."

I press my lips around his thick shaft and tease him the way I know drives him insane. I hollow my cheeks and bob my head on him. After a few seconds, he gathers my hair in his hands and helps glide me how he likes best. He pops out of my mouth, and when I lean forward to take him again, he stops me.

"No. I don't want to come yet, and I'm getting close. Lie on the bed and play for me. I want to watch." He helps me stand, and I get comfortable and find the rhythm I like the best until I'm breathing heavier and moving my hips around. I'm so close when he pushes my hand away and takes over with his mouth. It's not long before I'm pressing my hips into him and coming on his face.

He crawls up my body and pushes straight in. I moan and lift my hips up, pulling him in as far as he will go.

"You're my home, babe," he says and kisses me, leaving no space between us. He grinds into me as my next orgasm sneaks up on me. I shake under him as I wrap my legs tighter around his ass, holding him in me as his own orgasm takes over. His thrusts are sloppy, and his breathing in my ear sets off a mini orgasm. I shake under him and bury my face in his neck, peppering him with kisses.

He rolls over and pulls me to him for a tight embrace. "Let's get married at the ranch. We can have a small ceremony, just close friends and family." He plays with the ring on my left hand.

"Okay."

He rolls me to my back to really look at me. "Okay?"

I nod. "Yeah. Let's do it."

He's been dropping hints about having it on the ranch for months, and the more I think about it, the less I care. I don't need some big fancy wedding with all the bells and whistles. I used to think that was for me, but being with Tristan has shown me the simple things in life are what matter. I have him, William, and a family who loves us both. There's nothing else I need in my life.

"I love you, Tristan."

"I love you, too, Lana."

EPILOGUE

LANA

"It's bad luck to see the bride before the wedding. Get out of here." Beth pushes Tristan out of the door and locks it behind him. She turns to look at me. "Does he know nothing?"

I chuckle when I hear Tristan on the other side of the door, complaining that it's a stupid rule. I also may have snuck out really early this morning to see him for a quickie before I become his boring wife. Don't they say all the fun disappears once you're married? Well, that better be a lie. Our sex life has only gotten better since I moved out here almost a year ago.

I look down at my growing stomach and smile. Baby number two will be here in another few months, and she is making me crazy for Tristan. *Not that there is ever a day when I'm not. He can play me like a fiddle.* So much so, I can't keep my hands off him. Hence, the reason I snuck out this morning to see him. He stayed at his parents' house last night, and I thought it would be fun to get it on in the barn. We may have scared a horse or two with all the noise. Oops!

Beth helps me with my dress, zipping it up in the back, and

I breathe a sigh of relief as it goes up. I catch her eye in the mirror, and she smiles at me. She is already in her sea foam green dress and cowboy boots. No wedding on a ranch can be complete without cowboy boots, even though she fought me on wearing them.

"He's crazy about you," she tells me as she hugs me from behind.

I can't help but smile. "I'm crazy about him, too."

The first time Beth met Tristan, she pulled him into a corner and ripped him a new asshole. She dredged up our past and exactly how I was after he wrote me the letter all those years ago. She was with him for a while, and when we were finally alone that night, we had the most amazing make-up sex that ended in no less than three orgasms for yours truly.

Someone knocks on the door, and Holden is standing there looking amazing in a suit and tie. Beth gives him a once over and steps to the side to let him in. She may be taken, but she said it doesn't stop her from looking every now and again. And, according to her, Holden is a hottie with a body. She's not wrong. If he didn't end up hooking up with Molly, there's a chance we could have been together—a fact I remind Tristan of whenever he pisses me off.

I am really thankful for Holden, though. He's the one who had enough sense to get Tristan and me together again, and he kicked his ass in gear when he thought he'd lost me a second time. If I didn't stay connected to Holden all those years, I don't think it would have been possible for us to rekindle our romance.

"Everyone's waiting for us. You ladies ready to go?" he asks, extending his arm for me to wrap mine through.

"Where's my dad?"

"He's with your mom, John, and Liz. Your mom has all but

kidnapped William. She didn't want a moment without him, so I've been sent to bring you ladies over."

I chuckle and shake my head. Moving out here has been really hard on my parents, and they tried everything to get me to stay. It was a losing battle, though, since William came a month early. There was no way I could keep him away from this place. It's so magical. William loves being around the horses, and being able to drive him out to see the wild ones is amazing. He gets so excited as we watch them run.

We walk through the door, and Tristan is there, waiting to corner me since Beth hasn't let him come anywhere close to me. He grabs my arm, pulls me against him, and presses his lips down on mine. I vaguely hear Beth saying something, but Holden is too busy trying to drag her away. He puts his forehead against mine and holds me gently by my face.

"You look so beautiful, Lana. I can't believe this day is finally here."

"You're not supposed to be here," I tease.

"I couldn't wait to see you, and I wanted to give you something before you walk down the aisle. As far as I'm concerned, you've been my wife from the moment you told me about William, so screw Beth and her superstitions."

He pulls a little black box out of his jacket pocket and hands it to me. I gasp. Inside is a pair of pearl and diamond drop earrings that are exquisite.

"Oh, Tristan, they're beautiful." I pull one from the box to really examine it. "Where did you get them?"

"Your mom gave them to me to give to you. She wanted you to have something special, too, since my mom gave you the ring. She said she would have given them to you herself, but she wanted it to be special. That's why I was trying to get in earlier, so you could wear them today."

I take my earrings out and swap them for the new pair, which match the beaded belt that sits above my belly perfectly.

He kisses me quickly and says his goodbye so Holden can take us out to the field. I feel like a princess today. All eyes are on me when I step outside his parents' house to get into the truck. The place has been booming with business since the new cabins have opened. Once a month they host weddings here in the field. It turns out, a lot of people want to get married on a rustic ranch with wild horses.

I wave to a little girl who looks awestruck as Holden helps Beth and me into the truck. It only takes a few minutes to reach the place, but it's just long enough for the butterflies to start. I'm not worried about marrying Tristan. I've been waiting for this day for what seems like forever. I know I'm the luckiest girl in the entire world to be marrying the only man who has made me feel like I mean something.

Beth notices my hesitation while we're getting out and says, "There's always time to back out. No one would blame you, you know."

I roll my eyes. "Beth, trust me, there's not a chance in hell I'd run from this man. I can't wait to marry him."

"Then, get out of the damn truck already!" She shoves me, and I push open the door. I look over everyone's shoulders and see Tristan is in his place with Holden by his side. John, Liz, Mom, Dad, and William are all waiting for me so they can start their walk down. I tell them I'm ready, and the music starts to play. His parents start it off, and then my mom carries William, who is not happy to be in his little tuxedo. He has been trying to get out of it since we put him in it.

"You ready, pumpkin?" Dad asks.

"Yeah, let's do this." I link my arm with his and hold my bouquet as Beth finishes her short walk. There are only about fifty people at this reception. If Tristan had his way, he would have eloped with me at city hall long ago, but I couldn't do that to my parents.

They have a standing reservation once a month now, so we get to see them more often but still not as much as they would like. With little Ella coming soon, they have talked about moving out here. Not that I would mind in the slightest. They have no family back east, so why not? I've been trying to convince them of that since I found out I was pregnant again.

"Have you and Mom thought more about moving out here?" I ask as we walk past everyone standing for us.

"Your mother and I have talked, yes."

"And?" I say through a smile.

"We'll talk later." He gives me a big smile, and that's my answer. Yes.

We reach Tristan, and Dad shakes his hand then places my hand in his. It's all too surreal, being here with him. William has decided he's done and starts crying. We try our best to ignore him, but when I look at his chubby little face, and he reaches his pudgy little hands in my direction, how could I let him suffer anymore?

I take him from my mom and prop him on my hip as we say our I dos and give each other a simple kiss. I would have gone for more if it wasn't for the toddler on my hip.

"I now pronounce the new Mr. and Mrs. Tristan Ellis," the justice of the peace says.

We turn to face everyone, and they clap and cheer for us. That's it. I am officially Mrs. Lana Ellis, and I couldn't be happier. Our lives have been a whirlwind since the beginning, and for things to finally work feels so damn good. We were always meant to be; we just had to jump through a few hurdles along the way to find our happily ever after.

CHECK OUT MY OTHER RELEASES

Infatuated (Black Stallion Ranch #1)

Sugar and Spice: A Small Town Romance

The Publicist (Hollywood Lust Series #1)

The Playboy (Hollywood Lust Series #2)

The Starlet (Hollywood Lust Series #3)

Ever After: A Dark Suspenseful Romance

Sign up for my newsletter, Facebook group, or Tiara Tribe to stay up to date and have some fun!

Cara's Newsletter

Cara's Fictional Boyfriend Hub

Tiara Tribe

You can also check out my website to read snippets of upcoming books:

authorcarawade.com

ACKNOWLEDGMENTS

For those of you who have taken the time to read, and review my stories, my deepest thank you. Without readers there would be no writers.

Anyone who has been involved in this project, thank you. Thank you for letting me work though elements that weren't working and for offering advice on how to make it better.

It takes a village and you all are part of my village. I couldn't do any of this without you, and I wouldn't want to. Being a writer can be a lonely road, but with all of you in my life (virtual and real) you've made this a lot of fun for me.

I don't know what the future holds for me, but hopefully a lot more stories and a lot of fun! Stick with me kid. :)

ABOUT THE AUTHOR

Cara Wade is a daydreamer and a lifelong teenybopper. Boy bands forever! She would love to spend the day in the kitchen baking up sweet treats but hates doing the dishes after. When she is not writing (or suffering writer's block) you can find her reading, hiking, or relaxing by the water. She lives in northern Massachusetts with her loving husband.